PUFFIN BOOKS
LORI'S MAGICAL MYSTERY

Kartik Shanker is an ecologist, with a love for both mountains and marine life, and an occasional writer of children's fiction. If he had a choice, he would spend all his time visiting cool places, looking for sea turtles and diving off reefs or hanging out with his students, talking about science. He is the author of *From Soup to Superstar*, a history of sea turtle conservation in India. He is also the founding editor of *Current Conservation*, a magazine that combines art and science. His children's books include *Turtle Story* and *The Adventures of Philautus Frog*.

He lives in Bengaluru with his family, which includes the tree-shrew expert Meera, the tree-frog-like Vishak and their two tree-deprived cats. To know more about the author, visit www.kartikshanker.in.

Lori's Magical Mystery

KARTIK SHANKER

illustrations by PRABHA MALLYA

PUFFIN BOOKS

PUFFIN BOOKS

USA | Canada | UK | Ireland | Australia
New Zealand | India | South Africa | China

Puffin Books is part of the Penguin Random House group of companies whose addresses can be found at global.penguinrandomhouse.com

Published by Penguin Random House India Pvt. Ltd
7th Floor, Infinity Tower C, DLF Cyber City,
Gurgaon 122 002, Haryana, India

First published in Puffin Books by Penguin Random House India 2017

Text copyright © Kartik Shanker 2017
Illustrations copyright © Prabha Mallya 2017

All rights reserved

10 9 8 7 6 5 4 3 2 1

This is a work of fiction. Names, characters, places and incidents are either the product of the author's imagination or are used fictitiously, and any resemblance to any actual person, living or dead, events or locales is entirely coincidental.

ISBN 9780143429289

Typeset in Galliard BT by Manipal Digital Systems, Manipal
Printed at Thomson Press India Ltd, New Delhi

This book is sold subject to the condition that it shall not, by way of trade or otherwise, be lent, resold, hired out, or otherwise circulated without the publisher's prior consent in any form of binding or cover other than that in which it is published and without a similar condition including this condition being imposed on the subsequent purchaser.

www.penguin.co.in

*To Meera and Samira,
whose drongos inspired this story,*

and

*to Vishark and Squiddharth,
my fellow fans of fantasy fiction*

Contents

1
Smoke on the Water

10
What Can You Do, Ron Dongo?

23
The House of Owli

37
Le Kebab in the Sky

49
Eena Mina Mynah Mo

61
Boris the Loris

78
The Ballad of Don and Co-co

92
Welcome to Keralafonia

107
With a Little Help from My Friends

125
Notes

Smoke on the Water

One winter evening, the sun long gone behind the western mountains, a ghostly shape moved between the branches of the jamun tree. A cloud that moved quickly till it was a mere wisp and then gone.

From the crook of a branch of a tree, Lori watched, her giant eyes not blinking at all. Lori's eyes were her greatest asset. They made her seem innocent yet wise, naïve yet knowing. Grasping the branch with her tiny hands, she peered into the darkness and wondered what she had seen.

Lori's reverie was interrupted by a shrieking squall of night creatures. Lori was the shy, awkward one, and would really have preferred to be alone, but she couldn't stop the rest of the babbling beasts from imposing themselves on her. And whenever she was the first to find the insects, a bunch of bats and other creatures would descend around her to feast. From little Pip and Estrelle—the tiny insect-eating bats—to Sam, the large flying fox. For some reason, all the flying foxes were called Sam—Samson, Samuel,

Samantha, Sam.i.am, Sam.i.nathan. All of them.

The little bats were completely crazy. They shrieked—in clicks and squeaks and trills and chirps—and swooped in search of crickets and grasshoppers and other yummy treats that Lori would have been so delighted to catch. But in their frenzy they would leave several behind, half-dead or in shock. Lori, on the other hand, was a tiny but efficient cleaner-upper. She was compulsive about cleanliness. And when it came to food, she was so fussy, so finicky, you could even call her fastidious. She would walk slowly through the trail left by the bats, picking up each crunchy titbit and putting it away.

Today they were chattering about the insect explosion at the swamp. The dark and silent black water in the little valley to the south. Brilliant, Lori thought. She would go there too. Sam Fox was not interested. He enjoyed the company but he was vegetarian.

'All I want is some frude, dude,' he said.

Waiting for the frenzy to subside, Lori approached the flying foxes. 'Did you bats see a big cat?' she asked.

'Siruthai?' asked Sam, referring to Leopard.

'Dave?' asked the other Sam, thinking of Marten.

'Toddy?' mumbled Sam the Third, wondering if it had been Palm Civet.

'Hmm, no,' Lori said thoughtfully. 'It didn't seem like any of them. Too small for Siruthai. Too big to be Toddy. What other cat like that would be on a tree?'

Lori turned to the smaller insect-eaters, but she knew the cricket bats couldn't stay serious for very long. And soon enough, they were clicking and chattering around her, offering one batty suggestion after another.

'Maybe it was Panni Pig,' clicked Pip.

'Ha ha, that would make it a pig tree,' Estrelle tittered.

'Maybe it's a bird without wings,' said Pip. A snake with legs, a flying fish—they went on.

'Really?' said Lori with a long-suffering look. 'Is that the best you can do?'

Lori decided that she would investigate on her own. Mosey down to Myristica, the swamp—maybe she'd find some juicy insects left there for her. That seemed as good a path as any, with something to look forward to at the end of it.

Lori's eyes were large—bigger than her butt, in fact. She could see much of what went on in the still of the night. When darkness came like a cloud of ink, Lori's pupils just grew larger and larger. At first she could only see the shapes, but then the fuzzy outlines became as clear as crystal, and she could make out many different shades of grey. And, of course, she could detect the slightest movement in her field of vision.

'I'll see you all later,' she called out to no one in particular.

She picked her way through the forest, clambering carefully from one tree to another across a connected canopy, each branch leading to another and another till she was on the next tree, sometimes without quite realizing it. In some places, she had to pause and return because the branches led nowhere—all that lay in front was a big gap with a big drop to the ground. Every time she reached those dead ends, Lori sighed.

But she turned around and kept going. She took the route by the river that ran through the forest. It began way up at the top of the hill. Just a little collection of trickles and bubbles at first, it snaked together into rivulets and then gathered into a stream, which gushed into a happy body of water that gambolled downhill to the plains below. The river was her guide and caution. It drew a wavy line through the landscape, which she could always follow, always rely on to help her find her way home. But it also reminded her that it had another side—one that was not home, one she had never been to. And somewhere far away, the river drained into a little gulf of turquoise water that was dotted with pretty islands.

Lori did not even dream of going to those faraway places. She liked the little patch of forest that she had grown up in. When she was very young, less than a week old, her mother would leave her in a safe place and go out to feed. She remembered snatches of that time, when another loris—her father maybe—would come and visit, play with her. When she was about a month old, she'd started following her mother around. Struggling to keep up at first, she slowly got better and better at climbing and finding her way through the foliage.

And even more slowly, she started remembering the places she had been. Lori carefully recorded each new path that she found, mapping every twig, every bump on each branch, every wrinkle on the surface of every tree. She learnt the shapes of the leaves, the smell of the bark, the fragrance of the flowers in season, the way the stem forked and spread, arms reaching out wildly in every direction. She visited her favourite eating joints, the trees with the best menus, which harboured her favourite insects. And her favourite resting places, safe from the greedy eyes of a hungry hunter.

Till she had a map of her forest in her head: large branches were like motorways, bustling branches were like city roads, dusty twigs like country lanes. Now she could find her way around with her eyes closed—but she never did. Her eyes were always open, wary and wide. She remembered each tiny part of the little patch she considered home. That she possessed like a tree pixie.

She couldn't quite remember when her mother had disappeared. Initially, she'd clung to her like a leech, afraid to let her move more than a few branches away.

There seemed to be danger in every shadow. But as she'd grown up and got to know her forest, she was less worried about losing sight of her. At first for a few minutes, then a few hours. They were separated for many days at a time, and would meet again at a bug conference or a beetles' concert. But one day, Lori had realized that her mother had been gone for so long that she had nearly forgotten her. That maybe she would not see her again. That she was alone in the world. A loris, not so fast, somewhat slender and alone.

Lost in thought, Lori found that she had wandered to the lake, a little detour the river took to rest in the lap of the forest. A little palm-shaped depression in the otherwise rolling hill. The lake was large enough for Lori to only see the silhouettes of the trees on the other side. The water shimmered in the fading moonlight, a light breeze skimming over its surface. Lori meandered around the lake, hoping to find another good insect cache. Or if not, a good place to rest. She could feel the lake brightening and it would be morning soon.

And that's when she saw it again. The ghostly shape. There was no doubt this time that what she had seen earlier was real. Still the shape looked like it had been ripped from the fog and shaped into a catlike animal.

A ripple in the dew that drenched the dawn
And lay lightly over the water.
Like mist moulded by a potter.
Like a cloud captured.

But what was it? Too small to be a leopard, too large to be a cat or a civet. Was it the famed pogeyan—the mystical cat of the mist, the fantastic feline who vanished before he had been seen? Lori suppressed a giggle. She had clearly eaten a few dragonflies too many, or maybe the fruit she had picked had fermented. Everyone knew that the pogeyan was a myth, a long-tailed tale, a figment of the imagination of the loony fringe.

It strolled about the edges of the trees, rubbed its back upon a gnarled branch, let fall upon its back the dew that dropped from leaves, lingered above the languid pool, curled once around the corners of a forest fern and, seeing that it was a soft Sunday dawn, leapt on to the gloomy canopy and disappeared into the darkness behind.

Lori watched the feline-fog disappear and wished that she had someone with her. Someone she could have talked to about the strange smoky animal. Someone like Drongo. She had many friends in the forest, but none like him. Lori sighed. She knew she'd have to wait for the morning to tell him about it. She curled up in the cradle of a branch in a tangled tree and finally dropped off to sleep.

What Can You Do, Ron Dongo?

Lori awoke to the sound of Drongo whistling in the distance. The two of them made an unusual pair. But they got along. Where she was slow, Drongo was quick. Too clever by half, some said. She had never understood that phrase. If he was two clever by half, that kind of made him the regular kind of clever, no?

Lori and Drongo had a very special relationship. They only met once a day, just as Drongo was winding down and Lori was waking up. They both loved insects. Not loved as in I-want-to-hug-you-and-make-you-feel-special loved. Loved *eating* insects. Drongo was particularly obsessed, and would steal them out of his friends' mouths. As Lori awoke and started pottering about, she would hear Drongo imitate her call—a keen, high-pitched whistle. For a long time, she had thought it was one of her kind, another slender primate. Soon

she'd realized that it was the crafty Drongo, racket-tails dangling behind him in graceful swirls and regal waves, taunting the squat and slow creatures of the forest. But Lori had never felt jealous nor taunted. She'd watched with her large eyes as a socialite with opera glasses might watch the ballet.

And when bewitchment had given way to hunger and she returned to glean insects from the bark, she realized that she had hooked him. Every insect that escaped her careful paw, Drongo would pounce on. Initially, he'd tried to scare her into releasing one that she'd just caught. He'd swoop close to her and squawk—not the fluting calls he made to imitate the bluebirds, nor the song of the babblers. Just a loud, unpleasant noise to startle her. She'd fallen for it once and looked at him balefully with her giant eyes. So full of bale that the otherwise unflappable Drongo, the without-a-care, insect-stealing Drongo, had paused.

When they had decided to speak to each other, he had said, with just the gentlest air of pomp, 'My name is Don Wrongo, and I'm the best.'

'What can you do, Ron Dongo?' asked Lori, who was slightly dyslexic.

'*Don Wrongo*,' he emphasized. 'No one better than me at wronging other birds . . . you'll find out.'

'But I'm not a bird, Don Dongo,' Lori tried in vain.

Don Wrongo bristled.

'I'm a loris, Ron Rongo,' she said. 'A slender one, if that helps.'

Don Wrongo softened.

'You have a scary mouche, Ron Dongo,' she said. 'A bit frightening. Can I just call you Drongo for short?'

The rules were set then. Lori would glean insects off the bark, Drongo would swoop and sally and catch them in mid-air. There would be no stealing, and no eyes full of bale drowning Drongo in unfamiliar guilt.

'You glean, I sally,' Drongo would sing. Or sometimes with a wink, 'You sigh, I neeglee.'

'Oh, for the love of gordonflies,' Lori, dyslexic to her tiny toes, would reply.

And if he had been there that evening, Drongo would have been able to follow quickly, get close to the elusive animal and report back. He would have swished and sashayed back and forth, barking his pithy reports as he swept past her.

'Reporting large catlike animal,' he'd have snapped, swishing.

'Smaller than a leopard, larger than a leopard cat,' he'd have said, sashaying.

'I see spots, maybe—let me have another look,' he'd have sputtered, sweeping past her.

And then, strutting, he'd have summed up, 'Lori, my dear, it's a . . .'

But he hadn't been there to strut or sum up. And so, he paused thoughtfully when Lori had finished telling him her story. Lori had responded to his whistles with her call and he had come to seek her out, intrigued, even though they usually met only in the evening.

'This will require further investigation, my dear,' he said finally.

Drongo always lapsed into his best British accent when he was serious. His accent varied with his mood. As often as not, one could hear him say, 'Aye lassie, I dinnae ken that!' in a moment of Scottish cheer. Having grown up as a vagabond, Drongo had discovered an extraordinary talent for imitation. There was no voice, call or accent that he could not mimic. Whether it was the woodpecker, babbler, bluebird, tailorbird—Drongo could mimic them all.

Drongo had been born into a normal home, a collection of carefully crafted twigs woven into a cup that was secured to the branches around it with short bits of vine. He had good drongo parents who went out and caught insects and brought them back for the squeaking, screaming brood in the nest. But something wasn't quite right. Drongo remembered vaguely that one of his brothers was different from them. Brown where they were black. Spotted where they were smooth. Speckled where they were shiny. But more than that, he was quite the bully. Much larger, greedier and finally, much stronger.

One morning when his parents had gone out to catch insects, Drongo had felt himself being nudged. That would be his big brother making room for himself, hogging the bed. But no, this time he was being pushed quite forcefully. He turned to squawk angrily at his brother, and realized that his speckled brother was shoving him to the edge of the nest. Quite intentionally. There he tottered for a second, trying desperately to hold on. He couldn't believe he was being evicted from his own home. He squawked pitifully, waking his other siblings, but there was nothing they could do except join the clamour. And then, without so much as a hint of hesitation, the traitorous sibling toppled him over and Drongo fell.

Drongo flapped and flailed all the way to the ground, trying to slow down his descent, but he would have broken many bones anyway. Fortunately, he landed on a soft pile of old and mouldy leaves. He lay there, stunned. Finally he screamed and screamed, hoping his parents would come and fetch him. After a while, he started running out of breath. But more importantly, there were all kinds of strange sounds down there on the forest floor. It didn't seem like a safe place at all. Not like his comfortable cup in the treetop.

And when he saw something moving towards him, Drongo ran as fast as his little legs could take him to a little space under the roots—a little cave, dark and damp. But safe for then. Drongo realized later that he should never have survived. But he stayed in the root-cave for a long time. And enough insects wandered in for him to learn to catch and eat, so he was never hungry.

It took a long time, but he finally worked up the courage to walk out of his little home and on to the forest floor. It looked wide and open and terribly dangerous. He looked back up the bole of the tree that he had fallen from. It stretched upwards forever, and somewhere towards the sky was a nest he had called home. A twig snapped somewhere, the wind whistled through the leaves, sending several fluttering to the ground. Drongo was sad and terrified, and rushed back into his root-cave.

But as the days passed, he made small forays out of his cave and flapped about till he was able to fly short distances. He was clumsy at first—not just at taking off, but at landing, which was often awkward. After a few flaps through the air, he would come flailing down and topple over. He thought he looked foolish and checked to see if anyone was watching.

He still fondly remembered the first time he was able to fly up to a branch and perch there. Oh, he was so proud of himself! And then from one branch to another. When he could fly high enough, he flew back to his nest. It was the moment he had been waiting for. Been dreaming of every day. They would be so happy to see him again. He would be reunited with his parents and his brothers and sister. And he would tell them how his bully brother had pushed him out of the nest. And the family would reject that nasty bird.

But the nest was empty. His siblings had grown up and left, and his parents had gone too. So he flew away as well. Further and higher till he was flying over the trees one day, a sea of green stretching in all directions.

And he could go anywhere he wanted. And Drongo was happy that he had survived.

Drongo had to learn to fend for himself from a very young age. And so he was crafty. He heard the sounds of the forest and learnt to imitate them. He was charming and witty and could talk the feathers off a fairy bluebird, all the while calculating what he could get out of them. Soon enough, he acquired a reputation and with that, his name, Don Wrongo. Some said he was the cleverest bird in the forest. Drongo didn't think so—he thought he was the cleverest creature of all.

But the cleverest creature was foxed. And not in a Sam-foxed sort of way. Nor quite in a fantastic-foxed way at all. He was puzzled-foxed, flummoxed in fact. He was so lost in thought that Lori had to pull one of his whiskers to get his attention.

'Hey, Lori, cut that out,' Drongo said, returning to his normal guttural voice.

'Well, come back to earth,' Lori said. 'I'm hungry now. Wanna sally while I glean?'

This was very much the wrong time of the day for her to be feeding but she had been distracted the night before and hadn't eaten much. Drongo nodded, he was hungry too. But his mind was clearly elsewhere. Lori started working her way up the branch, looking under leaves, beneath the bark, in the crooks of branches. She found a beetle here, a caterpillar there. An insect would fly out and Drongo would swoop, ninja-like, and snap it up. And yet, here and there he missed some completely. So unusual.

Lori stopped.

'Drongo, clearly you can't get the mystery cat out of your mind. What do you want to do about it?' she asked.

'Find it,' he said.

'Find it and do what?' Lori wondered aloud. She had her own share of curiosity, but not one that involved organizing a search party for a vaguely cat-shaped animal.

'Come on, Lori. This could be some new kind of animal. Something new to our forest. Something that none of us knows about. Wouldn't that be exciting?'

Lori squinted at Drongo. 'Aren't there lots and lots of animals that we don't know about? All sorts of bugs and beetles that live in places we've never been,' she said.

'But this is a cat, Lori. Surely we know them all. A new cat in town. So cool!' Drongo persisted.

'You just secretly love mammals, don't you?' Lori teased him.

'And that, my dear, is why I hang out with you,' Drongo said triumphantly.

So they agreed that they would get a group together and search for the strange sight that Lori had seen. Once the decision was made, Drongo was all business.

'You get some sleep, my dear,' he said, his composure and British accent returning all at once. 'I will make some inquiries during the day, and round up some friends before our evening soirée. We can work out a plan then. Spread the word to the sentinels. Get some ears on the ground and some eyes in the air.'

Lori, who was a very literal animal, had visions of a forest floor littered with the ears of different animals—some pointy, some rounded, some flappy, some floppy, some furry—which was very gross. And of hundreds of eyes—green, brown and yellow—blinking at her from above the trees, which was a bit creepy. She shuddered and put the thought out of her head.

'Very well, Drongo. Go gather your troops. I will join you in the evening,' she said and ambled back to her roost where she would sleep through the day.

Drongo was on his own now, but not for long. If there was one thing that Drongo knew how to do, it was to get a party going. He was the ringmaster of a flying circus of birds who had insects on their mind. He knew how to bring them together—he had been studying them his entire life.

Drongo warmed up with the chirrup of the white-eyes. He added the whistle of Bulbul and, soon enough, she joined him. Drongo uttered a few chuckles and rattles. Velvet Nuthatch joined them, as did Scarlet Minivet and Blue Flycatcher. The group was growing now, and the commotion was getting louder, with all the birds chirping, whistling and tweeting up a storm.

Time to up the game. Drongo sallied and rallied the troops, getting them all excited and moving from one tree to another. Finally he heard what he wanted to hear—a group of babblers, birds that were quick to spot a predator and warn everyone else. He cleverly shepherded the group towards the babblers, eight or ten of them bustling about busily. Soon the mixed group grew larger and larger with Blue Flycatcher, Chloria Leafbird, Mr Smith-Barbet, Iora, Sunbird and Speckled Piculet (whom Lori always remembered as Pickled Speculet).

This was a good arrangement for all of them. Some picked insects off the bark, others off leaves, some caught them in the air, and a few kept watch because that was what they did anyway. Drongo was supposed to be a watchbird too, but he usually just scared the other birds and stole their food. The others weren't always sure they wanted to be around Don Wrongo.

Drongo marvelled at his ability to create the group. But he knew the group would eventually break up and move apart, so he had to act at the right moment. Drongo waited till everyone had eaten just enough, but were still caught in the buzz of being together.

'Hey, birdbrains!' he called out in his cousin Ashy Drongo's voice. The birds all turned to look accusingly at cousin Ashy, who unfortunately always looked guilty.

Then in his own voice, Drongo said, 'Fellow feathered friends, it has come to my attention that there is a strange animal in this forest, and I'd like your help in finding out what it is.'

'What kind of animal?' asked Babbler, the talkative one.

'Well, it was described as a smoky, cloudy catlike creature,' Drongo responded.

'Someone has been imagining things,' said Leafbird, tittering. She was jealous of Drongo because she could whistle and mimic too, but not nearly as well as him.

'I have it from a very reliable source,' Drongo said, drawing himself up.

'From whom? Your friend Lori? Monkey in slow motion! She must have turned her head too slowly,' said Mr Smith, who tended to be a bit ruder than he needed to be.

Drongo turned to the bird who had spoken. 'Mr Smith,' he said, 'you would do well to watch your tongue. Lori knows your tree hole, and she fancies the occasional egg for dinner. And Chloria, I'd be happy to teach you how to mimic better if you would be so kind as to mimic silence for now.'

Barbet grumbled and Leafbird mumbled, but they both fell silent. Don Wrongo was not to be trifled with.

'Birds, you are the eyes of the forest,' Drongo said. 'Keep a look out and report anything strange you might see. Pronto Toronto.'

'And what do we get out of it?' Barbet demanded.

Drongo's whiskers twitched. 'Maybe I won't wrong anyone for a whole week,' he said. 'No surprise alarm calls that make you think Jungle Cat is crouching behind you.'

Barbet shuddered. Drongo's false alarms would make his cheeks go white. The birds all chirped and tweeted and agreed that this wasn't a bad deal. Soon enough, the party broke up. This whole cloudy-cat story was mildly interesting but not something that any of them with their tiny brains could keep track of for long.

Drongo was perfectly aware of that. There was another thing he needed to do. Sidling up to Bob the babbler, he said casually, 'You know this is a top-secret mission, right? And I'm putting you in charge. Now, don't go around telling everyone about it.'

Bob Babbler lowered his beak and winked at Drongo. 'Not a babble from me,' he said. But he would soon be walking around casually as though he had no interest in conversation. Pretending that he was just pecking around, looking for a worm. No, sir, he had no interest in talking, nothing to talk about, no top-secret stories to hide. But Bob Babbler would slowly get more and more anxious, and finally the words would break from him in a torrent.

'Fine, fine, fine, I know you're dying to know, and I know I promised—but I'll tell you. Just this one time . . .' And he'd tell the bewildered birds around him the story of the magically disappearing mystery creature. And of course, he'd repeat it to just about anyone else he ran into. Drongo knew there was no better way of letting *everyone* know, and he smiled at his own cleverness.

The House of Owl

Several days passed before Drongo and Lori met again. Babbler had done what he did best, and pretty much everyone in the forest knew about Lori's story. Many thought that was all it was—a story. Something she had dreamed, or made up maybe. But Drongo would not give up.

'We need a higher power,' he said. 'We have to go to the Greatest.'

'What? I thought you were the greatest,' Lori said sarcastically.

'The cleverest, my dear. I am the cleverest,' Drongo clarified. 'We are going to meet the Greatest.'

He led Lori through the forest, flying on ahead as she ambled behind, through avenues that were spooky and scary with shadows. The trees were taller too, and Drongo led on till they came upon a large arjuna tree. She looked up to see the branches spread like an arboreal palace. It towered over the trees around and struck her with awe. Whose house was this, she wondered.

Who were they here to meet? Drongo directed her to a comfortable spot halfway up the tree and said, 'Now we wait.'

And wait they did. The sun disappeared behind the hill, leaving a sickly pink sky, pale freckles of cloud far above. The evening light brought a buzz of insects and Lori was tempted to eat some, but Drongo would not let her. 'You must be still and silent,' he said. The darkness was eased by an almost-full moon. A chapatti badly rolled by a child.

Thin clouds soaked in the moonlight and let a warm glow fall upon the tree, where the gentle rays bounced off the leaves and fruit and lapped against Lori's head. The hours rolled by. Lori was getting thoroughly bored, hungry and irritable, when all of a sudden a large object blocked out the light and darkened their world.

M. Owli descended in a crescendo of flapping wings, his large, powerful strokes creating a gust before him.

'Who lurks in the House of Owli?' he thundered.

'Chill, Mr O,' said Drongo. 'You're going to knock us right off the branch.'

'I can be delicate,' said Owli. 'You know, flit like a fruit fly, flap like a fairy. No, that doesn't sound right. Float like a bumblebee, fly like a mayfly. Flail like a fairy, fry like flutefly. No, I give up—you know what I mean.'

'Oh, for the love of gordonflies!' Lori said, instantly wishing she hadn't spoken. This was an animal that ate her kind. Why would Drongo bring her to meet him?

'Oh, I got it, I got it, I got it! *Float laike a burrrfly, sting laike a beee*,' Owli sang and turned to look at Lori. Lori shrank behind a branch.

'Calm down, Kebab,' he said, seeing Lori cower. 'You'd taste good with some masala, but I just ate two rats. Mmmm.'

Lori made a face.

'Hey!' said Owli, seeing her expression. 'We have to eat too, you know. If we starve, do we not die . . . of hunger? Can't get over this anti-meat propaganda that's going around these days.'

'Focus,' Drongo would've liked to have said to the eagle-owl. The Great Horned Owl, some called him. The Greatest Living Being, Owli liked to say. And the Greatest had large talons and a vicious curved beak. So Drongo was careful with his words. You had to be sometimes.

'O Great One, the Greatest One. We need your assistance,' he said instead.

'I don't assist,' said Owli. 'Advise occasionally. Yes, I advise a lot even when no one wants it. And I would recommend that you seek elsewhere for assistance. See, there—that was advice. I told you.'

'Better to have the vice in advice than be the ass in assistance, eh?' chuckled Drongo.

Lori sighed. If this was going to get anywhere, she was going to have to brave the creature that gave her night terrors. Between Drongo's wordplay and Owli's wordiness, they could spend all night talking around each other without ever coming to the point. Without once listening to each other or ever wondering what the conversation was about. Where it had started, where it was going to end.

Such talk made Lori's head spin. So she scrambled forward between the two and turned her enigmatic eyes on Owli, who had quite a striking pair himself. But where hers were liquid, his were piercing. Where Lori's look went straight into your heart and turned it to mush, Owli's gaze went straight into your head and turned it inside out. When he wasn't talking about himself, that is.

Now he looked at her. 'Oh, look, the kebab presents itself. You really are lucky I'm not in the mood for a morsel.'

'Mr Owli. The Greatest. Mr the Greatest Owli,' she said. 'Only you can help us resolve the great magical mystery of our forest.'

Owli could not resist flattery. With him, a little pandering to the ego could get you everywhere.

'I saw a strange, smoky catty creature a few days ago,' she continued. 'It disappeared before I could tell what it was. And we haven't seen it again. Drongo has told all his daytime friends but none of them have any idea what it is.'

'And you think I can help because . . .?' Owli asked.

'Well, think about it, Mr O,' Drongo said. 'It must be active at night. Lori saw it at dusk and again at dawn. So it must be nocturnal. Hence, thus and therefore, we should be looking for it at night. And Lori can move only so fast. No offence, Lori.'

Owli thought about it. And when Owli thought, the world slowed down. For him. For others, it was pretty much the same—a bit boring, though, to watch an owl think. Not greatly different from watching paint dry.

For Owli, on the other hand, it was like watching the world come into focus. And when it did, he would clearly see all the pieces of the puzzle come together, their complexity made simple, and he could distil the vagaries of the world into one wise thought. And it was awesome when that happened. More often than not, though, Owli's mind would simply wander off and be a-thinking of rats and mice and other such items of food. And when it returned from its travels, he would just make something up on the spot that could pass for wisdom. Fortunately for him, hardly anyone could tell the difference.

'Your movement is the continuity of great facts,' he pronounced.

Unfortunately for him, Drongo was not just anyone. 'Mr O, what kind of flibbering gibberish is that?' he asked.

'Your heart is inside visible timelessness,' Owli said.

'Uh-uh. You are random-babbling, Mr O. Get a grip!' Drongo said crossly.

'Infinity is the wisdom of reality?' Owli tried again.

'Mr Owli, I think Drongo is right. This is not making any sense,' Lori chipped in.

'Awright, awright. I got nothing,' Owli said in resignation. 'What did you have in mind?'

'Now you're talking,' Drongo said. 'We want you to do a recon and report back to us. Just a quick flyover above the forest at night. A little stealthy survey.'

'No can do, Drongo,' he said—which Lori heard as 'No can drool, Dongle' and wondered what on earth he meant.

'Oh, come on, Mr O.' Drongo started working his charm. 'With your magnificent wings and your extraordinary eyes, you can find what no one else can. Not for nothing are you the Greatest!'

'Oh, very well, Dee-rongo. Don't think you're fooling me with flattery,' Owli said. 'Fool me once, you know I'm a fool. Fool me twice, I'm two fools. But I'll never be . . . never mind.'

Lori sighed. This was going to be a long night. 'There's not much of the night left, Mr Owli,' she said. 'We'd really appreciate it if you could take a look around.'

'Just one fly-around, okay? Don't wait up, kids,' Owli said and, spreading his enormous wings, took off, leaving a drumbeat of sound that seemed to echo long after he was gone.

M. Owli floated like a butterfly over the canopy, his laser-like gaze stinging the trees. He flew east towards the dry lands, where the trees were sparser. Short and thorny, bristling against the harsh land. Owli enjoyed hunting there. It was more open and he could easily spot faraway prey from his favourite giant rock that he'd sit on to survey the landscape. He'd fly out there when he wanted something slightly different for dinner. A gecko, an agama, a gerbil. And Owli's mind wandered thinking of the times he had caught one unsuspecting animal or another.

Not much to see today, he thought. Some blackbuck, handsome even in repose. Some sleeping spotted deer at the edge of the forest. A troop of bonnet monkeys, huddled like statues, almost in 'see no evil, hear no evil, speak no evil' poses. Only time of the day that's true of a monkey, Owli thought and smiled.

He flew on till he reached the edge of the forest. He could see fallow fields stretching into the distance and the place of people beyond. He knew there would be lots of rats there but like most of the animals in the forest, he did not go there unless he absolutely had to. And so far, he had never absolutely had to.

And then he saw something. A streak of spots that moved stealthily behind the trees. Was it Lori's smoky surprise? He glided in closer and realized that it was just

the restless leopard. Sneaky Siruthai, as he was known. Careful not to get too close, Owli asked him if he had seen anything strange.

Siruthai growled, his voice like a saw, 'No strange animals here in the forest, all the weirdos are in the village. Fat cows, strangely coloured cats, bizarre dogs—yum by the way—and don't even get me started on the people.'

Other than the Bonnets, Siruthai was one of the few forest animals that moved in and out of the villages with ease. He was not welcome there, but Siruthai was a cat burglar. He could slip into any village, grab a dog or a small goat and be out before anyone found out something was wrong. He could live deep in the forest, or at its edge, or in the sugar-cane fields, or even in the attics of houses sometimes. And when people heard a sound—a scraping or a sigh, a brush or a breath—they knew that something lurked. But every time they turned to look, Siruthai was not there.

'Will you let me know if you see anything?' Owli asked politely.

'Sure. Wanted dead or alive? I can take care of it,' Siruthai said nastily.

Siruthai had not always been like this. Once, long ago, he had gone through a very difficult time. He would not hunt in the village very often then, but he had been tempted by a succulent street dog and had fallen into an abandoned well. Siruthai could climb any wall, jump any fence—but as he was in water and the walls were slick with moss, he could neither climb nor jump. He swam there till he was spotted by a child who was passing by. Soon a group of children gathered, and they threw sticks and stones at him. He continued swimming around, anxious and afraid, but there was nothing else he could do. Any of those brats was little more than a meal, which added insult to injury.

Some bigger people came, he was hit by something sharp and he went to sleep. When he woke up, he was in a box and being taken somewhere. He remembered being released far, far away from home. He had trouble hunting because the forest was new, and he couldn't find his way around easily. And it seemed the animals were more skittish there. The hungrier he got, the angrier he became. But Siruthai had a compass deep inside him and he followed its direction every night. He caught a goat here, a dog there and even eyed the occasional child—but they were usually surrounded by others.

Months later, he reached home. By now he was used to eating village food. Forest food tasted great but village food was easier to catch, if a bit fatty. And often it was tied up or fenced in. People are strange, he thought. And then, that he was still angry at them and wanted to get his own back.

'Siruthai, don't kill anyone unless you're going to eat them,' Owli said. 'That's not right. And please don't eat this smoky secret till we've had a chance to talk to it.'

Owli flew on. He circled south to the river and then flew west towards the western mountains. In the distance, they rose up dramatically, but he would not go that far. The forest below grew denser and taller. Owli caught movement out of the corner of his eye. He turned to look but it was gone. Probably a mouse scrambling to safety after hearing death-on-wings approach. Owli would have paused to search but he really wasn't hungry. He was comfortably full for now.

Further on, he heard nightjars and frogmouths calling. He considered asking them but didn't think they noticed much. He was about to give up for the night and return home, when he heard a deep *hoo-hoo* echo through the forest. A wild *hoo-hoo-hoo-ha-ha* moaning that could only be the doing of one creature. Baba Brown the owl, his nemesis.

Baba Brown was large and aggressive like Owli. The two of them were the heavyweights of the owl world. But they were as different as pork and peas. Owli was from the east, Baba from the west. Owli's ear tufts stood upright and cocky. Baba's slinked sideways and sinister. Owli's legs were feathered and majestic. Baba's were naked and menacing. Owli was young and brash. Baba was older and brooding. And long ago, they had fought a violent battle.

It had all started over food. Brown Babu, as his followers would call him, was a strict fish-eater, and believed that meat-eaters were the bane of the forest. He had gone around preaching his gospel of fish. 'I will make fishermen of you,' he had said to one and all. And one day, he had taken on the young M. Owli.

'Your mouse-eating habits will be the death of you, they will be the death of the forest,' Brown Babu had said. 'You eat without meaning, without mercy.'

'Well, that just sounds fishy to me,' Owli had said.

'When all the mice are gone, owls will die of loneliness of spirit. For whatever happens to the mice, also happens to us,' Brown Babu had thundered.

'What are we, mice or owl?' Owli had quipped.

'Do not talk to me thus,' Brown Babu had roared, enraged. 'Don't you know who I am?'

'One big brown mouse, looks like,' Owli had said, smirking.

Baba, who could not take it any more, had come at him strong, wings spread like an albatross's, talons flashing in the moonlight. But Owli was quick with a trick, and sidestepped him in a flash. Where once there was owl, now there was just space. Baba attacked again and Owli rolled back with the punch. Both hooted and howled as they flew around.

There was a great rumble in the jungle and all the other owls had turned up to watch this great contest. Scops with his fine collar, Owlet in his pinstriped suit, Barnie all snazzy in white and all the other owls and owlets. They were all a little fed up with Baba Brown's sermons, and cheered on the young contender. Woody with his ghostly *whoo-ah-whoo-oo-ah*, Owlet all delicate and dainty (barring her screeches).

'Owli, Owli, Owli!' they had all chanted.

Baba Brown flew at Owli again and again. And Owli dodged left, swerved right, ducked down, hovered above, this way and that and this again. When Baba caught him with a left swipe, Owli retreated in a flurry of feathers. This went on and on—Baba attacking, Owli ducking. Baba chasing, Owli avoiding. Over and over, till Baba was exhausted.

And at that moment, Owli turned towards his tired opponent and launched a lightning attack. He hovered above him for a split second, more eagle than owl, and then in a flash of wings and talons, descended on him. In mere seconds, one owl had taken a terrible beating. Baba Brown knew the fight was finished. Within minutes, the vanquished owl had retreated and flown away.

M. Owli had been the toast of the forest. All the other owls had proclaimed him the Greatest. And he had strutted around and basked in the attention. Baba had moved away. He had grown older, lost most of the feathers on his head and become fat. But Owli knew that he had not forgotten. Or forgiven. That he was still a force to contend with. And so, Owli gave the moaning a very wide berth and returned home.

'I'm sorry, Kebab and Donko,' he said when he got back. 'Searched high and low, but no sign of nothin' strange.'

'Nothing?' asked Drongo, deflated.

'Not a shadow,' Owli replied. 'Oh, wait, that's not true. I did see a shadow,' he said, getting their hopes up. 'But it was only Siruthai, sulky as ever,' he finished.

Lori's eyes gave away her disappointment. Somehow she had thought that Owli would solve this deepening mystery. Perhaps it was too much to expect that Owli would have found such an elusive animal on his first flight. He was out every night and, sooner or later, he would surely see something smoky, somewhat strange. And then they would know what she had seen. They asked him to keep an eye out and he said he would let them know if he saw anything. Somehow, though, Lori knew it was not going to be that simple. Interesting things never were.

Le Kebab in the Sky

The nights turned warm and the days were hotter. The sun beat down every day, turning the world into an oven that baked the earth. The animals sheltered in the shade, cooled off in caves, slept in burrows, waiting for the rain. Waiting for someone to turn on the tap that would bring relief.

Lori slept in a shady nook of a leafy tree, and didn't come out till very late each evening. This meant that she missed seeing Drongo for many days. In any case, they had heard nothing from Owli. The search party birds had long forgotten about their mission. There was no more tweeting, no whistling, not even any babbling.

The days passed in a haze of shimmering heat and it seemed to Lori that the entire forest had slipped into a summer slumber. Late one afternoon, Lori awoke suddenly. A fat blob of rain had emerged from a cloud, dropped on to a tall tree, come slip-sliding its way down, rolled off a leaf and splashed on to her brow. Rousing herself, she moved through the branches and looked out.

Dark storm clouds had gathered. For days now, the earth and the sky had traded waves of heat, water shivering through the air, till it had all gathered to form a grey ghoul in the sky. The approaching deluge announced itself with pomp and ceremony, like a powerful emperor. Drumbeats of thunder, fireworks of lightning. Moments later, the droplets clamouring in the clouds—crying to be released—burst free and fell upon the forest. Lori moved back into her hollow and waited for the summer shower to pass.

These storms were like tantrums, a child stomping its feet for a few minutes. Not the long, sulky drizzles of winter, not the steady deluge of the monsoon, nor the thunderous rage of cyclones. Lori loved the smell of damp earth that accompanied the first showers of the season, which told her that the heat was soon to end.

And stop it did after an hour or so, leaving a relief of rain-drenched trees, their curls hanging by the sides of their heads, wet and happy. From the top of the hill, the valley looked as though one was viewing it through a freshly washed windowpane.

This would be a good time for insects. And so Lori started bustling about. It was still early in the evening, and there was a good chance that Drongo would still be up. Soon enough, she heard him call out to her.

But Drongo was in one of his moods. He didn't feel like talking. Not in his own voice, and much less in that of the many others he could call upon. He'd been feeling like this for days. He'd even stopped going to the parties.

Lori knew that something was wrong.

'Wassup, Drongo dude?' she asked, trying to imitate him and failing miserably.

Drongo remained thoughtful. Finally he said, 'I guess I can't stop thinking about that darn creature.'

'Why do you care so much, Drongo?' Lori asked. 'I've almost forgotten about the foggy feline, it's fading fast from my memory.'

Drongo hesitated. There were many different answers that he could have given. It was the spirit of the chase, curiosity about a cat, passion for knowledge, altruistic assistance to potential prey. But in truth, it was none of those. And he knew he couldn't lie to those large, liquid eyes. Limpid pools in which lies would drown.

'Lori, I've never given up on finding my family,' he said finally. 'And I just—just thought if we found something really big, really dramatic . . . then *everyone* would know, and maybe my family would hear about it. About me.' Drongo paused, his voice caught in his throat for a moment. 'And then we could be together again,' he finished.

'But everyone already knows you, Drongo,' Lori said in a quiet voice.

'Only in this forest. I want to be famous everywhere! Maybe they moved really far away. Maybe I wandered too far.'

'Oh, Drongo,' Lori said. 'I'm sorry. I didn't know it still bothered you so much. You're so cool and clever and funny.'

'Don't you ever miss your family, Lori?' Drongo asked.

'I guess I do, but I think I knew that my mum would leave when she did. I wish I had spent more time with my dad, though. He seemed like a fun guy.'

'Maybe you'll see him again one day, Lori,' Drongo said kindly.

'I don't know, Drongo,' Lori said firmly. 'I think I am quite lucky to have had parents. As were you, even if it was so brief. Most of the folks in the forest have just one, and many others have none at all. But I know how you feel, Drongo. Let's go find that darn animal!'

'Let's go, Lori,' Drongo said. 'Not quite hand in hand, but certainly hand in glove. Or glove in wing. Or something.'

And so they set off again, the odd couple. They paused occasionally to snap up an insect or two, but not for too long. Drongo felt a new energy, and he darted around looking for new routes, new avenues through the trees. He found good lookouts where he could perch and steal sharp looks in different directions while he waited for Lori to catch up. Drongo knew that they might not actually find this misty mystery, that it might not be the magic wand that would help him find his family. But at least he knew now why he was looking.

Tomorrow he would have a party. He would remind all those birdbrains about their promise to him. Wait, he could only remind them if they remembered what he had talked about in the first place. He would have to start over as if he were talking to them for the first time. Send Babbler on a secret mission again. Get Warbler to compose a song—a hit single perhaps. Of course, Drongo knew he would have to compose it himself.

'Stop!' Lori yelled suddenly.

Drongo stopped.

'Look,' she said, pointing at a shadow behind the branches ahead. Her eyes adjusted and she added, 'Oh, it's just Rusty.'

Rusty was another strange creature; no one quite knew whom he was related to or where he'd come from. But as far as Lori was concerned, just as avoidable as all the other carnivores.

Drongo could not see that far in the fading light and flew up for a closer look. Sure enough, it was Rusty, the spotted cat. Drongo looked back and couldn't even see Lori under him. He was impressed that she had sighted Rusty from such a distance. Drongo's brain started buzzing. And something wicked in his eye flickered.

'You know, Lori,' he said, flying back to her, 'I think we have a problem with our strategy.'

'And what might that be?' she asked, dreading the inevitable. Another Drongo scheme. Whom would this one wrong?

'Owli has eyes that are designed to catch movement at night. But of small animals. That he wants to eat.'

'Yes, and so?'

'So maybe he is flying past this creature and just isn't seeing it,' Drongo explained.

'Maybe . . .' Lori said. 'But what can we do about that? We can't change the way his eyes behave.'

'No, we can't,' said Drongo, 'but if he had eyes that look for predators at night . . .' He paused. 'Eyes that have seen this particular predator.'

'What eyes have . . . ?' Lori started. 'Oh! Oh, no, no-no-no! You are not giving him my eyes!' She stopped. 'And what does that even mean? How would you *give* him my eyes?'

Drongo, devilish as always, kept looking at her. Lori, literal as ever, looked back blankly.

'Oh, come on, Lori,' Drongo said finally. 'Owli could carry you around the forest and you could look with your amazing eyes. Amazing, astonishing eyes!'

'Drongo, you know your silly flattery doesn't work on me. However many kinds of fools I may be. That's the craziest idea I've ever heard,' said Lori.

'But think, Lori,' Drongo said. 'Imagine the number of times you've wished that you could fly like me. This would be your chance. And maybe we'll even find your catlike creature.'

Lori was tempted by Drongo's daring plan. He certainly knew how to press her buttons. Of course, she was only a bit larger than a very large button. This was the craziest idea that he had ever had. At least the previous ones hadn't involved handing her over to someone who considered her food. Who called her Kebab and smacked his lips.

'What if he forgets what he's doing and thinks I'm a rat he just caught?' asked Lori.

'We shall feed him till he is stuffed,' Drongo said, delighted, 'so that food is the furthest thing from his mind.'

'Oh, for the love of gordonflies,' Lori said, but weakly now.

As daft as the whole scheme sounded to Lori, they set off to the House of Owli again. And waited for the Greatest. And when he arrived, Drongo tempted him with talk of ratatouille and mousse, till Owli was hungry again and went out for another snack. Then another, and another, till he was too full to move.

'Fill me once,' he said, swaying, 'I'm a fool. Fill me twice . . .'

'Look, Mr O,' said Drongo, 'I'm glad you appreciate the five-course meal, but we want you to try something for us.'

Owli was too dreamy to care.

'We want you to carry Lori on your search and recon today. She can look out for the mystery animal. Two pairs of eyes being better than one and all that.'

Owli sat up. He hadn't bargained for this. But he was full and happy and thought, *what the hey, what could possibly go wrong?*

'You'll have to be gentle, Mr O,' Drongo said sternly. 'I want my friend back with all of her intact. And if you get distracted or hungry, think of the mouse you just ate.'

'Don't remind me of that!' Owli said, groaning. 'And don't worry, I'll take care of the little kebab. She might make a nice snack one day.' And before Drongo could threaten the wrath of his wrongs upon him, Owli held up a wing and said, 'Just joking, Don, just joking.'

And so, gripping her wee arms gently in his not-so-tiny talons, Owli took off with Lori. With the first rush of air around her, Lori felt a rush of fear as she had never experienced before. As they climbed rapidly and the tree fell away, she thought that she might have left her heart on the branch below. For several seconds, she could not breathe. But then she felt her heart within her thundering like a drum, and she calmed herself down slowly. Feel the force, she thought.

Fear gave way to exhilaration and she marvelled at being able to fly through the air. High over the trees, she pretended in her mind that she was flapping wings and flying herself. For what seemed like hours, she enjoyed that feeling of weightlessness, like a leaf in a summer breeze. Like a moth in a maelstrom. She imagined she could go anywhere in the world. Reach for the moon, maybe.

Her reverie was broken by Owli's voice. 'Flying high, high—le kebab in the sky!' he drawled in his deep baritone. 'Snap out of it and start looking for your foggy feline!'

'How did you know?' she asked.

'Well, you know, my first time, had a bit of a head rush too,' Owli said.

So Lori looked with her giant looking-glass eyes, searching for the slightest sniff of a smoky shape in the shadows. And though it seemed like the silliest project ever, she did it because she knew how much it mattered to Drongo.

Owli flew high over the valley till the trees seemed like pins. He flew along the river till they seemed to flow like it. He flew her through the forest, swerving to avoid the branches that sprang to make an obstacle course. By this time, Lori was loving it. She nearly squealed with delight when he swooped through the cassia, the golden rain tree rich with yellow blossoms, and swung up just in time to avoid the mahua branch that loomed in front, the sticky smell of its flowers flooding her senses.

And Lori looked and looked. To the east they went and then west. Along the river and away from it. By the lakes and swamps and patches of rock. It seemed like they had been flying through the forest for ages. Lori had completely lost track of where they were. Even if they had been flying over the trees, she would not have had much of an idea. Unlike Drongo, she knew the forest better from below. And a very small part of it too. And now, after the long, meandering flight, she had absolutely no idea where she was.

'Maybe we should head back, Mr O,' she said.

Owli agreed. He flew into a clearing and swung upwards to get his bearings.

The attack was swift and sudden. With a wailing *woo-woo*, Baba Brown was upon them. In his shock,

Owli raised his talons to defend himself—a moment that would remain forever etched in his memory. Could he have dodged left, jerked right, dropped down to the safety of the trees? He would never find out.

All he knew was that he had dropped Lori. From far above the treetops. She was so tiny, he thought. He had felt the little bones in her arms as he had held her. Bones he could crunch with the tiniest flexing of a talon. *Oh, le kebab*, he thought. *You could never survive the fall—you're going to break every bone in your body!*

In the same moment that would remain etched in Owli's memory, Lori's mind went blank. A moment before, she had been flying fearlessly. A moment after, she was falling, terrified. But the moment in between was gone as if it had never existed. As she sank through the air like a stone in water, she had one last passing thought. This is how little Drongo must have felt.

Eena Mina Mynah Mo

Drongo was getting impatient, waiting for Owli and Lori to return. He made short, undulating flights from one branch to another, swishing his rackets in annoyance. The summer sun was quick to heat up the day. The light would soon be too bright for Lori. He knew she liked to spend the day in the shade. As eager as he had once been to send her on this mission, he now began to have qualms. What if something had gone wrong? What if, in an absent-minded moment, Owli had forgotten that his passenger was a friend, not food?

And then he looked up to see Owli flying towards him. Relief was replaced with dread when he realized that Lori no longer dangled below. He was certain he knew what had happened. When Owli landed, Drongo attacked him with no thought for himself nor for the matter that the owl was ten times bigger, twenty times heavier and maybe a hundred times stronger. But Owli did not fight back. He just hung his head in shame and covered it with his wings.

After Drongo had exhausted himself, he cried out, '*What did you do?* What did you do to Lori? Did you eat her?'

'What? NO! Are you crazy, Drongo?' Owli protested. 'I wouldn't do that!'

'Then what happened? Where is she?'

Owli paused, reliving the painful memory. 'I dropped her,' he said.

Drongo looked stunned, speechless for once. Owli explained what had happened, how he had been attacked by Baba Brown, how she had slipped from his grasp. That they had fought again and, though Owli was younger and stronger, he had been distracted by the thought of Lori crashing to the forest floor. The older owl had chased and ripped at the younger one, until Owli had been in danger of losing his life. Finally he'd dropped through the trees, and managed to evade Baba. But, in all that chaos, he had completely lost track of where he had dropped Lori. He'd waited till dawn and flown around looking for anything that was familiar. The clearing, he remembered. But he could not find it.

'I'm sorry I attacked you, Mr O,' Drongo said. 'I just can't believe she's gone.'

'That's okay, Drongo. I know the two of you are really close friends.'

But Drongo felt lost now. Was there even any point in searching for Lori? There was no way she could have survived the fall.

'But what do we do now?' he asked.

A great sadness came over M. Owli. He did not even feel like jabbering his general gibberish, which was his standard response to stressful situations. He had never felt quite like this before, and wanted to get away from it all. Go somewhere far where no one would disturb him. To the smooth and soothing rock of comfort that rested atop the mountain. He had often wished it would come to him, but now he would go to it. And before Drongo could say another word, Owli bid him farewell and flew away to the mountain.

'Never to return,' he said in leaving.

Drongo sat there, stunned. He felt all the cleverness drain out of him. It had been his scheme, after all, that had led to this. How could he have been so foolish? To talk Lori into this madness? To put her life at risk? All so that he could satisfy his curiosity. So that he could find his family whom he barely knew and hadn't seen for years. When all along, she had been the best family he had ever had. The one he had needed the most.

Drongo was depressed for days. He wandered around in a stupor and barely ate anything. But there were sudden sparks of anger. How could the world have treated him so badly? First, evicted from his own home, abandoned by his family. And now, through a cruel twist of fate, his best friend had been snatched away. Day by day, the sparks accumulated till they became a raging fire.

Drongo had been wronged. Now he would be Don Wrongo again, wronging the world with a vengeance. During his youth, he had hung around with a bad mob of mynahs. They were a rough crowd, bullying other birds big and small. They thought nothing of taking on serpent eagles and brahminy kites.

The leader of the gang was a tough bird called Major Mynah. And Drongo's gang name was Mynah Surgery, for the cuts and nicks he could inflict with his scalpel-like tongue. They had caused a reign of terror back in the day, during which they wreaked much mayhem.

Eventually Drongo had found it too crass for his taste. He preferred to wrong by cleverness. With surgical precision rather than bludgeoning brutishness. With a thousand cuts of the knife rather than the dull blows of the hammer. And so Don Wrongo had struck out on his own.

But now he sought them out, for he wanted to think no more. It would be refreshing to harass a cat, harrow a crow, harangue a kite. A frenzied mob chasing after a victim without a moment's thought of why or what. And after several days of searching, he found them on the edge of the forest, by the side of a road.

'Oh, look, it's Mynah Surgery,' said the one with a tuft, Dee Mynah.

'Yes,' Don Wrongo said huffily. 'I did say I'll be back.'

'But you didn't say when,' said He Mynah, a large, macho male, certain that this must clinch the argument.

'And you didn't say where,' squawked Def Mynah atonally.

'Or why,' chirped Gee Mynah, whom almost no one knew.

'You thought you were too good for us,' said Hey Mynah.

'I was wrong to think I could be wronger than you,' Drongo protested. 'Please, let me be part of the gang again.'

But Major Mynah seemed almost embarrassed. 'Oh, we don't do that any more,' he said. 'We've gone straight now. The mob has disbanded.'

'What!' exclaimed Drongo. 'How could that happen?'

'It was a mynah miracle,' Major Mynah said somewhat sheepishly. 'My lady convinced us that we should change our evil ways.'

'Your lady?' Drongo asked in disbelief. He hadn't noticed, but there was a shy and pretty bird next to Hey Mynah.

She sidled up to Major and locked wings with him. 'I'm B-flat Mynah,' she said.

'What do you do now?' Drongo asked.

'We go around singing songs of love and peace. You must give up the scalpel, Mynah Surgery. Your sharp tongue has not changed the world. Sing with us! The tune is mightier than the word.'

Drongo was disgusted. Even his attempts at wronging the world were falling flat. B-flat, to be precise.

Drongo wandered around muttering to himself. He was in a state of despair, when distraction came in the form of Mina Mouse. Mina, who had fled her home and arrived all aflutter in their forest, and was talking about the dark secrets of Baba Brown.

Mice were terrible at keeping secrets. And staying away from cheese. Now, Mina had a friend from whom no secret could be kept. And so she told Tina. Who shared with Sheena. Who roomed with Reena and whispered to Veena and lingered with Leena. Who knew Nina and joked with Gina who danced with Dina and bumped into Bina. And so the story had spread by word of mouse.

And to Drongo the news had come. To Drongo the news had run. And through Bina and Dina and Gina and Nina, who knew Leena and Veena and Reena and Sheena and Tina, he had traced the word all the way back to Mina Mouse.

'What's this I hear about Baba Brown?' he asked her grumpily. Drongo was still not entirely sure why he was interested or cared. Perhaps deep down he held Baba responsible and wanted him to be punished in some way.

Mina Mouse told him her long story of trauma and terror. That Baba Brown had gone quite mad. After his last battle with Owli, he had turned into a raving lunatic and gone about attacking every creature in sight. No one was safe any more. Mina Mouse had barely escaped with her life. She had hidden under a rock for days, shivering in fear, while Baba had wreaked carnage outside. Mina had waited till the sun was high above—surely Baba would not hunt in the middle of the day—and, braving the numerous other predators that lurked, had scurried as far as her little legs could carry her.

But all Drongo heard was 'yadda-yadda-yadda'—or, to be precise, 'squeakie-squeakie-squeak'. Drongo was bored to tears and couldn't believe that he had worked himself up for this. So Baba seemed a bit more anxious than usual—he had always been an edgy owl—and so had changed his diet. So what? He wished he could disconnect this mouse.

'But he doesn't even eat them!' she said tearfully. 'Just kills them and leaves them there.'

Okay, that was definitely strange. But now Mina was saying something about eyes, lovely limpid eyes. Surely she couldn't still be describing Baba Brown?

For a heart-rending moment, Drongo was reminded of Lori. 'What's that?' he asked.

'What's what?' she asked, looking around suspiciously.

'What was that you said about eyes? Whose eyes are you talking about?' he asked.

'Oh, the lovely lady who'd just moved in next door to me. Lovely lady with beautiful big eyes,' Mina said. 'And she didn't eat mice.' Which was the deciding factor in the friends department for Mina.

But Drongo was frowning. This sounded like Lori all right, but then it could have been any old relative of hers. 'And when did she move in, Mina?' he asked.

'Just a week ago, right next to my house,' she said, then sighed. 'But I don't have a house any more. And neither does Roger.'

For a moment, Drongo wondered who Roger was, but there was something far more important. 'Are you taking the mickey out of me?' he asked, wondering if someone could have put her up to this elaborate and cruel prank.

'I don't know what you mean, Drongo!' she squeaked indignantly.

'I just lost everything—my life, my savings, my career in spelunking. Everything! What would I be making fun of you for? I'm telling you, this lissom lass moved in next door—and she seemed lost, to be honest.'

'Did this neighbour tell you her name?' Drongo asked, barely able to believe what he was hearing.

There was the longest pause while Mina considered this (or thought about cheese). And then she said, 'Hmm, no. Yes . . . but—hmm, no.'

'Oh, for heaven's sake!' Drongo snapped and stomped his feet. 'Take me to your home,' he said. 'I need to meet this friend of yours. Could be a friend of mine.'

Mina looked at Drongo like he had lost a few screws. 'Go back?' she squeaked. '*Go back?*' she squealed. 'Never. Never ever. *Never never!* Why don't you just roll me in gift-wrapping paper and mail me to the owl!'

Drongo was highly tempted. But he shook his head regretfully. 'Don't worry, Mina,' he said. 'I have a plan.'

Now, Mina had not heard that line before, for if she'd had, every single instinct would have told her to scurry into her nest and stay there for a really long time. But she had not. And yet a shiver went up her spine, and every single instinct told her to scurry into her hole and stay there for a really long time. Which she did.

'I have some friends,' Drongo called out as she fled, 'with a very *particular* set of skills.'

Eena Mina Mynah Mo, he thought. The game was afoot.

Drongo found the Mynah troupe again without much trouble.

'Major Mynah, my main mentor,' he said, 'I come to you in my hour of need.'

'What song will soothe you, Mynah Surgery?' Major Mynah asked. B-flat Mynah beamed, thinking she had recruited one more talent to her ever-growing band of birds.

'Not a song, old chap,' Drongo said. 'More of a dance.'

Major Mynah looked perplexed.

'A dance of the sort that we used to dance together,' Drongo said with a wink.

'But we don't . . .' started the major. Then he paused and thought of his glory days. So many missions accomplished. And now all they did was sing psalms. It was enough to make a grown mynah cry. He looked Drongo in the eye and asked simply, 'Is there a target?'

'Would I come to you without a target? Major, I ask you, would I?' Drongo asked.

'Oh, no!' cried B-flat Mynah. 'You cannot go down that road again. We have all given it up. Let us hold wings and sing.'

'Go on then, what is it?' Major Mynah asked Drongo, ignoring B-flat's pleas.

Drongo told him. Major Mynah's eyes widened, then narrowed. And he turned around and asked his troupe, 'What do you think, boys—shall we create some mayhem?'

The mynahs were shaken. It was so, oh-so tempting.

B-flat Mynah started singing suddenly, and clapping, and chanting, all at the same time. 'Lay down your wings,' she sang to the rest of the mynahs. 'Stay here and sing!'

The singing was okay, but the chanting was too much. That settled it. The mynahs had been stirred. They muttered their apologies to B-flat and prepared to leave.

Def Mynah said suddenly, 'I will stay back and sing! We cannot leave B-flat alone. And I am too old to mob!'

B-flat couldn't believe her luck. Of all the birds, Def was the one who couldn't sing at all.

'Don't leave me, Major,' she implored.

But the major was resolute. 'The mission comes first, darling,' he said. 'We will return to sing songs of victory with you.'

And off they flew, following the suddenly jaunty racket-tails of Drongo. In the distance, Drongo could hear the fading sounds of B-flat Mynah's stubborn song. He thought he heard Def's tuneless whistle too. Then B-flat snapping at him. Then silence.

Across the forest they flew, and towards the mountain with the hump on its head. On its slopes were meadows that were carpets of grass. Beyond that, the forest flanked by rhododendrons.

'Go to the cinnamon tree,' Mina had said, her mind drifting when she remembered the smells. 'Past the valley,' she'd said, 'is where Baba Brown hunts.'

As they flew towards the mountain, Drongo had some misgivings. He could not really be sure that Mina had met Lori. It could have been any one of her cousins, or uncles, or aunts. Or, for that matter, the niece of a second cousin of a distant aunt.

Drongo faltered. Hadn't he wronged enough already? Lori was gone. Owli was gone. Was he leading the mynahs to an early demise?

But then Drongo remembered Lori's baleful look. 'And you never came looking for me?' he could imagine her asking. What kind of friend would he be if he didn't even try to find her?

Drongo flashed his racket-tails like a conductor would his wand. And the band fell into formation— Dee Mynah and He Mynah brought up the rear, Gee Mynah and Hey Mynah flanked Don Wrongo, and Major Mynah led the charge.

Into the valley of death, rode the six angry birds.

Boris the Loris

Falling through the air, Lori remembered little Drongo. And, instinctively, she flapped and flailed. Which did very little to slow her descent because her arms were not wings. But her hand snagged on something which sagged just a little under her weight and cut her palm. Lori grabbed a vine, her lifeline, with both hands and held on, not quite believing that she had not crashed on to the ground.

For a while, Lori just hung there, suspended, dazed and confused, unsure of what had just happened. Eventually, she looked around and realized that she was hanging from a liana that stretched across two trees. What luck! She was not used to this sort of gymnastics. Not for her were the leaps of faith that langurs made into the void only to find a branch at the other end. But she moved to safety, one hand after another, until she reached the tree. Finally, she was there and rested her head against a leaf.

What an adventure! Flying with Owli. Falling from the sky. And staying alive.

What a story to tell Drongo, she thought. And then her euphoria evaporated as she realized that she was completely and hopelessly lost. Far, far away from home. She was a small, slow-moving animal. Her chances of ever returning home were remote. Surely she would never find her way back, she thought. Or ever see Drongo again.

Lori sighed. But she knew that she should try and find a safe place to rest. She set about looking for a suitable tree. But everything there was strange. Every bump, every turn, every twig, every fern. So far from home, she may as well have been on another planet. Not an animal stirred. And even if one had, she would not have known who it was. She didn't have a single friend there. Lori had never been so unhappy.

And then she smelled a waft of something that caught her attention. The fragment of a fragrance familiar. That tapped lightly upon her senses and tickled a memory.

She couldn't quite place it, but she knew it was something that she had smelled before.

Curious, she moved towards it and, soon enough, she came upon an enormous cinnamon tree. There was no doubt about it. Lori knew the tree. Something about the smell of the bark, the feel of the leaf, the curve of the trunk. She couldn't have possibly known, and yet it had drawn her to it. Lori climbed high, the exertions of the day having caught up with her, and she curled into a ball in a safe little crook and fell asleep.

Lori slept for a very long time. All of the excitement had taken its toll. She slept through night and morning and afternoon and evening. She was woken by a squeak. She scowled. 'Drongo, stop pretending you're a mouse! And it's not yet time to get up,' she was about to say.

Then, all of a sudden, she remembered what had happened the night before. And she was overcome with loneliness and despair. Then she came out of her comfortable cubbyhole and found herself face to face with a little mouse.

'OMG!' the mouse squeaked. 'Where did you appear from?'

'From the sky,' Lori could have said, but that wouldn't have made any sense. Instead she said, 'I dropped in, kind of, from above.'

Which was not that much better. The mouse looked at her like she had seen a ghost and said, 'Oh. My. God. Are you—?'

'Am I what?' asked Lori, perplexed.

'God. You know.'

'No, no!' said Lori. 'I'm just from a different part of the forest.'

'Well, then, what scary eyes you have, Grandma!' said the mouse.

Lori looked at her, not knowing quite how to respond. She blinked slowly once or twice, casting her calming spell on the mouse.

'Okay. Now that I think about it, they are not so scary. In fact, they are pretty lovely,' she said, peering closely.

'Where am I?' Lori asked. 'Can you tell me which part of the forest I'm in?'

'Which part?' asked the mouse. 'The part that I'm in, of course. Which other part would it be?'

Lori realized that was not going to help.

'And the part that the big, nasty owl lives in,' the mouse continued. 'You want to watch out for him. Of course, he only eats fish, but you never know.'

Lori stayed near the mouse for a few days, who kept up a running commentary on the goings-on of the forest, much of which was of little interest to her. She explored a little bit on the first day, but it was so much harder to remember paths now that she was older. When she had been young, she had just needed to walk a twig-trail once and it had become etched like a map into her head.

The next day, the mouse just disappeared and Lori was alone again.

Lori liked the comfort of the cinnamon tree but she knew that she had to move on and explore. Early the next morning, she climbed to the top of the tree and peeked out. She was in a little cup-shaped valley, and the slopes stretched upwards towards grass-covered mountains. But they all looked the same. More or less. One of them had a hump on its head. Home could be east or north or south. She was pretty certain it wasn't west.

She came across Panni Pig rooting around for pretty much anything he could find.

'What's up, Panni?' Lori asked, desperate to talk to someone.

Panni looked up from the ground, his nose covered with gunk. Peering at her, he said, 'Hey, Lori, what are you doing here?'

'Visiting,' she said vaguely. 'And what about you?'

'Visiting,' he said truthfully. Pickings were lean at that time of year.

'Did you just come from the east?' asked Lori, hoping to get advice on the way home.

'*Flabahabaht*,' said Panni, his nose buried deep in the soil.

'What?'

'*Flahgaghawaart*,' she heard this time.

'Panni,' she said crossly, 'take your nose out of the mud for a moment!'

Panni looked up. He was a large, bristly animal with the attitude of an elephant in musth, a bull in a ring. Smaller animals kept well out of his way. As did big ones like Karadi Bear and Gaur Bison the boss. Even animals that would be happy to eat him, like Siruthai. And even the elephants avoided him if it seemed like he was angry. Which he always was.

So the look was enough. But it always went right through Lori. And in return, he got a glass of cool. Which coursed through him and made him feel like a pink piglet. He shook himself out of the reverie and reverted to his customary cussedness and said, 'Tell me, tuber. What can I do for you?'

'Panni, do you think you can point me home?'

'Of course,' he replied, then added, 'not.'

'Don't you know where you came from?' Lori asked, losing hope.

'Oh, no, I go where my nose takes me,' Panni said, flaring his nostrils for effect.

'Where does it take you?' Lori wondered aloud, by now just curious.

'Where *doesn't* it take me, potato?' he said to the tuber with oversized eyes. 'Oh, the warm aromas of the north; the sweet, sticky smell of the south; the bamboo scent of the east; the fishy odour of the west.'

Lori tried to recall the smell of home, but Panni's words made no sense to her. Warm odours and sticky aromas, or was it the other way around? It just wasn't helping.

'I follow the fragrance with my eyes closed,' Panni was saying, by then lost in memory.

'Don't you bump into things?' Lori asked, still as literal as ever.

Panni frowned at her. 'That's their problem.'

'But how do you know that you are not lost?' Lori persisted.

'We are guided,' stated Panni, 'by the Great Pig in the Sky.'

And that was just that. Panni returned to his rooting and Lori to her lazy Sunday afternoon. By evening, Panni was exhausted and lay in a pool of mud, his corpulent body heaving gently with every breath.

'How's it going, Panni? Did you find anything to eat?' Lori asked. Or dig your way to China, she thought to herself.

Panni grunted. 'This place is awful!' he said. 'Nothing in the forest but a few chewy snakes. Nothing in the grass at all—not even a snake!'

And then he returned to his lumbering slumbering.

The rains returned. And with them, the forest came alive. The streams bubbled and burst from their banks. The frog orchestra began to play, with croaks and chirps and clicks. Some Lori recognized, others sounded new. And the snakes were out of their burrows, feeding on the frogs.

And of course, there was a bonanza of insects. At least she didn't have to worry about food for a while. One day, as she tracked a swarm, she came across the clearing where she had landed. The liana that had saved her life lay stretched across the gap. Who had heard these trees fall, she wondered.

Could this be the way home? Beyond the clearing, the forest seemed to slope downwards to the lands below, but she couldn't be sure. As she tentatively put one hand on the liana, Lori suddenly felt a tingle down the back of her neck. Her pulse was racing.

What had the mouse said? This was the part of the forest Baba Brown lived in. Which made sense—it was not far from here that he had attacked Owli. She had not seen him again since that day, but he must have been around somewhere. A fish-eater maybe but, as Mina had said, you could never be sure. And then the mouse had disappeared. That was ominous.

Lori turned very, very slowly. Which was normal, since that was all she could manage. And found herself looking at a large pair of eyes no more than a few feet away. Larger than hers, less liquid certainly. For a moment, her heart stopped. But this was no owl. This was like looking at a reflection. In a crazy mirror that distorted the image a bit. A slightly scuffed-up mirror. The loris that was looking at her was a bit more grizzled, a shade scruffier. His eyes were harder, but something soft behind them glimmered.

'I wouldn't do that if I were you,' he said.

'Who are you?' Lori asked.

'Name's Boris,' he said. 'Boris the loris.'

'Hello, Boris. Would you know if this liana leads to the forest that leads to the plateau where the river runs?' Lori asked, grateful that she could talk to a creature that would understand her.

'It certainly does, young lady. Now, what is your name and why do you want to know?'

'My name is Lori, and I think that's where I came from. I need to find my way home,' she said.

Boris chuckled. 'Home is where the food is. That way does lead to your "home" but there is a narrow passage between the two hills that is currently being guarded by a crazy owl. I wouldn't risk it. Plenty of food here.'

'But I must get back to my friends, Boris. They will be worried sick. I'm sure they think I'm dead!' Poor Drongo, she thought. 'Isn't there any other way out?'

'Well, there is another way out west, and then one can circle back around the mountain with the hump on its head.'

'Could you show me, please?' Lori asked. Boris resisted. But where Drongo had charm, Lori had the irresistible liquid eyes.

Boris sighed. In a way that reminded Lori of someone.

'Okay, then,' he said. 'I'll take you up to the passage in the west and show you the path that may lead to the place that you think is where you came from, which for some reason you think of as home. After that, you're on your own.'

'Deal!' said Lori.

Boris met Lori at the cinnamon tree the next evening. He looked up and down appreciatively. 'I remember this tree,' he said with a hint of a smile.

'So do I,' she said, realizing instantly that it was true. And yet it could not be. Boris shot her a look but did not say anything more.

They set off together, heading west, unaware that in just a few hours, a posse of birds would be flying in formation in search of this very valley.

It took them nearly all night, but they reached the western slope. Boris led her upward till the trees grew shorter and finally ended. Beyond, the grassland stretched all the way to the top of the mountain. Lori had never seen such a lush and lovely field before. It looked beautiful, a sea of green. But it was as dangerous for her as the sea was to an animal that could not swim. She ventured out, just a few feet into the fronds. How dangerous could that be? Boris watched disapprovingly, bearing a baleful look that Lori thought seemed familiar.

'Let's get going,' he said.

'Just a minute,' she responded. 'I've never seen anything like this.' And she went on. A foot further in the grass each time.

And on and on till she was in the middle of the meadow, green and golden in every direction. A dull cloud muted the moon and cloaked the carpet. It was quiet, but like a moment's silence in a music hall. And slowly the thump of percussion began.

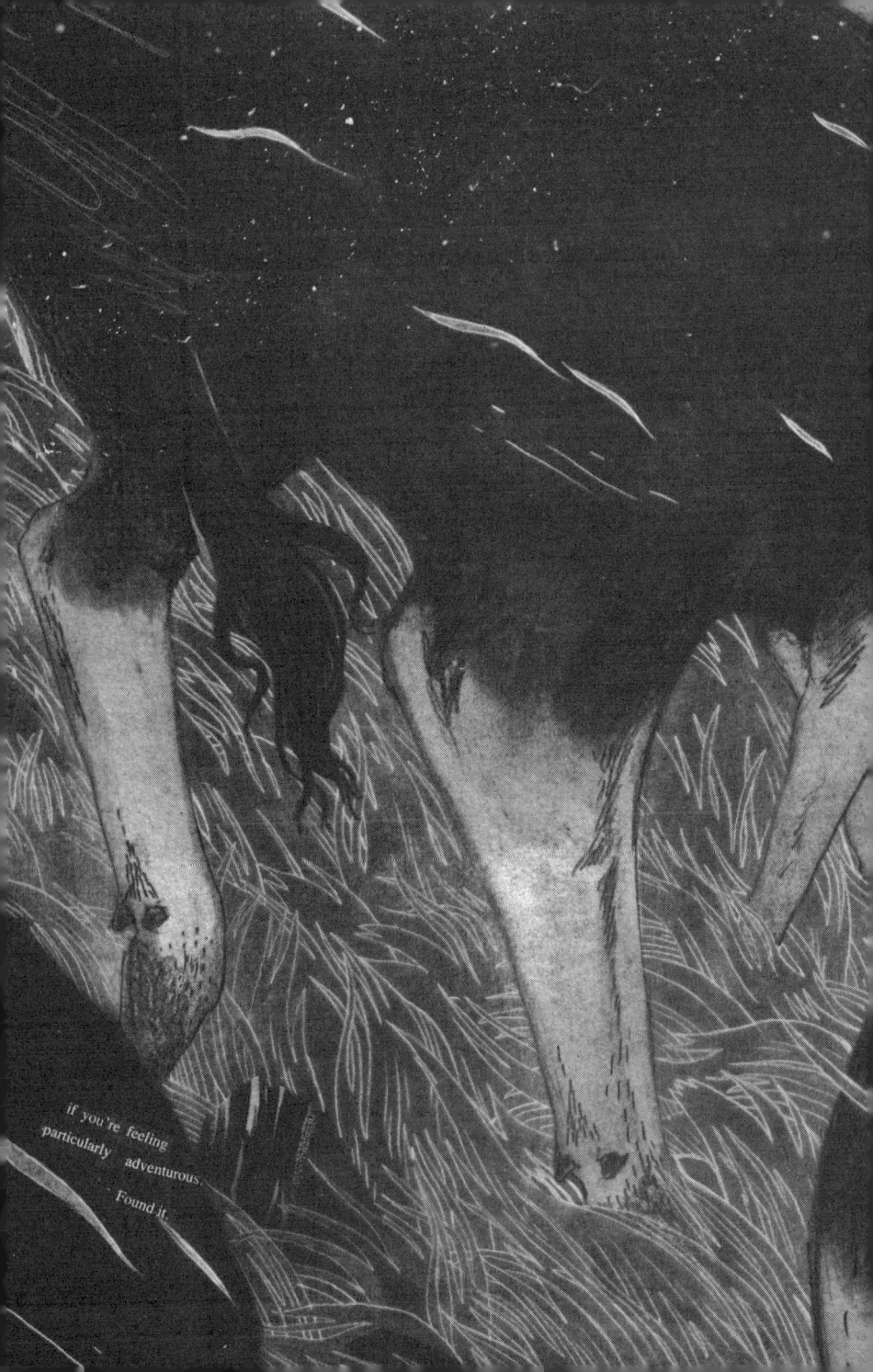

Lori wondered if the forest had hidden the sound from her all these years. That perhaps the drumbeats were part of this open world. But she turned and saw in Boris's fear-stricken eyes that she was in danger.

Lori looked up the hill and saw the shapes of the lumbering beasts, gaur in the mist. They were trotting down the slope towards her. Then thudding, then thumping, then thundering. If they kept this up, she would be stomped into a small smudge in the mud. The drums grew louder till her ears were ready to burst and, just as a hoof appeared in the air above her, she felt a body—an arm—drag her behind a tiny rock. The hooves thundered past, their bellies glistening above, swept up the hill beyond and were gone.

Lori lay shaken to the core, her head still ringing with the sound of bison hooves drumming the ground. Boris lay next to her, inert. She turned, horrified that he had been hurt. But he was just exhausted.

'I am so sorry,' she said. 'I didn't mean to, I didn't think there would be danger! I certainly didn't—'

Boris waved her off. He couldn't quite remember the moment when he had rushed to save this crazy animal—a moment of irritation but, in that same second, also of an irresistible urge to rescue her. But he did remember lying against the rock, limp with relief that she was okay.

'Forget it,' Boris said. 'Let's move on.'

To the west ran a stream through a narrow passage between the hills, flanked by a strip of forest.

'Those are the only trees on this route, Lori,' Boris told her, pointing at the passage. 'We'll have to cross through them carefully and hope that no more danger lurks. There will be nowhere to escape to if we're caught there.'

'You don't have to come with me,' Lori said. 'Just tell me which way to go after I cross.'

Boris paused, but then he remembered something. The smell of cinnamon.

'I'll take you across. And then we'll see,' he said.

They set off again, down the narrow riverine patch. A finger of forest snaked down the valley and joined the jungle below. They stayed close to the stream, but they could see the open grasslands on both sides. Lori knew they were still exposed. But somehow she felt safe with Boris beside her. It was a feeling she could not explain.

They were halfway across when Lori saw it again. The apparition that had led to all this. She stopped dead and pointed, but Boris had already seen it. The catlike

creature was bathed in moonlight as it strolled through the grassland at the edge of the trees. It leapt gracefully on to a rock and sat there statuelike, as if carved from a cloud. And as if it sensed eyes upon it, the creature turned and looked at Lori. Lori did not know if she'd been seen but, a moment later, the magical mystery melted into the meadow and was gone.

'What on earth was that?' Boris asked.

'I don't know, but that was what brought me here,' Lori answered. And then she told him her story. The deal with Drongo. The flight with Owli. The fall. All of it. And as the words tumbled out, she realized how crazy it seemed. And wondered whether it had all really happened.

'In the talons of an owl, hmm?' Boris asked. 'That takes a fair bit of courage. You're a spunky little one!'

'No, I think I just have crazy friends,' she said.

'And you still want to go back to them?'

'Yes, but first, do you think we could follow that animal?' Lori asked.

'Wouldn't you rather just go home?' Boris inquired, surprised.

'Well, having come this far, seems a shame to go back without finding out for sure,' Lori said.

Her friends had no idea she was still alive. It would be so cool if she went home and gave Drongo the fantastic news that she had solved their case! Boris wasn't quite sure why he was helping this strange little loris. But it seemed like he could barely help it.

'I have some friends that I think could assist. But they live down there,' he said, pointing to the slopes that dropped down precipitously.

Lori looked down the hill fading into the darkness below. How much quicker it would be if Owli could just fly her down, she caught herself thinking. And then—*what*? Nostalgia for being at the mercy of an animal that could eat her? That might drop her in the middle of nowhere? She felt bad that she wasn't appreciating Boris quite enough.

'C'mon, old man,' she said. 'Let's go find your friends.'

The old man didn't seem offended by her manner of addressing him. Which surprised him. And much later, her.

The Ballad of Don and Co-co

The sun was still young in the sky as Don Wrongo perched upon a branch and watched the bird on the other side of the crossing. The bird was bigger than Drongo and had a gruffer voice. Nothing even mildly mellifluous about it. She looked like the giant jungle crow that Drongo had seen at the edge of the forest. And kept a safe distance from. But this bird was smaller and had an elegant grey collar. Perhaps he should strike up a conversation, Drongo thought. It was time he did something; he was getting impatient. It had been two whole days since he and his mob of mynahs had breached Baba Brown's defences and invaded the valley.

They had swept into the narrow passage between the hills. All seemed quiet, and for a moment, Drongo had thought that Baba Brown might have left. But just as they thought they were through, the owl had risen from the trees and attacked them. Maybe Mina Mouse was right after all, Drongo thought—this owl was definitely deranged.

But nothing that the mob of mynahs could not handle. Gee and Hey wheeled off to the left and right while Dee and He swooped above and below. Major Mynah flew right at the owl and swung aside to avoid him at the very last moment. Round and round they flew, harassing him from every direction. Baba swung this way and that but every time he fought off one mynah or two, another would hound him from behind. Soon his head started spinning. Hadn't there been another bird too? A darn drongo?

But Drongo was long gone. In the chaos, he had dropped down quietly and flown along the edge of the trees into the cup of the valley. He had found a little gap in the forest with a liana criss-crossing the clearing. He flew down and perched at the edge of the forest. He waited a while.

Not far away, Major Mynah noted that Drongo had found his way into the valley. He whistled to the mob and they quickly led Baba in the opposite direction, letting him chase them for several minutes. Once they were far from the valley, they had disappeared into the trees. Mission accomplished.

Drongo had found the cinnamon tree without much difficulty. It towered over the forest like the mouse had said. But search as he did, there was no Lori there. He called to her with whistles and tweets, at dusk and then at dawn. But there was no answer. Nothing to indicate that she had ever been there.

The following day, Drongo found a couple of minivets and questioned them. Sure, they had seen a loris around, but he was a grumpy, grizzly old one. Sounded nothing like Lori. But they hadn't seen him for a couple of days. They thought it was strange too—he had been there for a long time. Maybe he had left, maybe he'd been eaten, they said. But Drongo just didn't believe that.

He'd flown to the western edge of the valley and found the riverine strip that fell to the plateau below. Drongo considered his options. He could go back home, but he would run the risk of facing Baba on his own. He could surely hide in the forest and sneak back, but the thought of returning without finding out what happened to Lori just did not appeal to him. He didn't know what dangers lay in the lands below. He figured that he had nothing to lose. No family to return to, and no Lori either.

Drongo had made his decision. He wheeled in the wind and flew down and down and down, till the mountain was towering behind him. As he descended, he looked out at the plateau, a great forest stretching out in front. Here and there were little gaps with plumes of smoke rising out of them. As the ground levelled out, he stopped at the edge of the forest and decided it was time to rest.

The next morning, Drongo had awoken early to the sounds of the forest. The birds he heard were very different. It would take a while to learn their language, to mimic them till he could get them to do what he wanted. Drongo may have been far from home and on a very different path, but he couldn't help wanting to call a party—it was just instinct. That would have to wait till he could make some calls.

He would explore the smoke that he had seen from above, Drongo decided. He flew around till he found a clearing. *Ah, people.* A small village in the forest with a handful of huts. Tiny fields. And on the other side of the path, a black bird with a grey collar. And as different as the bird sounded, Drongo wanted to talk to her.

'Hey, crow,' he said. 'Where you goin'?'

The crow turned to see this tiny bird with the long coat-tails, a smart alec, a whippersnapper. She did not have time for this nonsense, and ignored him.

'C'mon, crow,' Drongo persisted. 'I'm new here and I need some information. And sure, there's a bunch of other birdbrains around, but I wanted to talk to someone smart. Someone with intelligence.'

The crow looked at the bubbling black bundle of words and was intrigued. 'I'm sorry, little black bird,' she said. 'I wish I could help you, but I've got my own problems to deal with.'

'Well, hey, now,' Drongo said, 'you've found the right bird. I'm a problem-solver par excellence. Maybe I can throw some light on it?'

'Well, then, how come you have a problem of your own, genius?' she retorted.

Great point, Drongo thought, and was delighted that he'd found a fellow bird as clever as him. *Almost as clever*, he corrected himself.

'Good point, Ms Crow,' he said. 'Perhaps we can help each other. A fresh perspective on two prickly problems.'

'Maybe,' she said.

'Excellent. My name is Wrongo. Don Wrongo. But you can call me Drongo,' he said with a dip of his whiskers and a swish of his tail.

'My name is Crow-co,' she said. 'And you can call me Co-co.'

'What's your problem, Co-co?' Drongo asked.

'Well, my partner, Kau'a, and I had a fight and now he's gone. I've been trying to find him for several days. We hang out near the edges of the village and so I've been going from one to the other. But no sign so far.'

'That's an amazing coincidence!' Drongo said excitedly. 'I'm looking for a friend too, Co-co. But why did you fight with Kau'a?'

'Well,' said Co-co, 'we had a nest together. Such a perfect nest—high up in the fork of a tree. I spent several days gathering twigs and sticks and weaving them all together. And then I did the interiors, lining it with soft wood and dead leaves. I laid several eggs in the nest and a few weeks later, all of my chicks were born. Kau'a and I would feed them constantly.'

'Sounds idyllic,' said Drongo, who hated these happy-family stories.

'It was,' said Co-co. 'Till one day, we came back and found that all of them except one had fallen out of the nest . . . We looked all over for them but they were gone! Our largest chick was still there, though, and so we looked after him till he left home. But Kau'a was so upset that he just flew away and never came back.'

Drongo was speechless.

'Maybe it was my fault,' Co-co was saying. 'But I want to build another nest with Kau'a. I'm sure we can do a better job of looking after the chicks!'

'Oh, Co-co,' said Drongo, reliving the painful moment of his childhood when he had been pushed over the lip of his nest, 'it's not your fault.'

'That's nice of you to say, little bird with an opinion—but someone has to take the blame. It was negligence.'

'No,' said Drongo firmly. 'It wasn't negligence. It was the big chick. The one you found when you returned. He pushed the others out.'

'That's not possible!' Co-co said angrily. 'Why would you say such a thing? He was the blackest of them—so beautiful!'

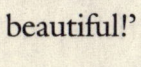

'Co-co, I was pushed out of my nest by my brother too,' said Drongo firmly. 'He was larger than us, stronger. And one day, he threw me out. I survived but I never saw my family again.'

'But why would he do that? *Why would my chick do that?*'

'Well, I'd always wondered about that,' said Drongo, 'and so I did some research. Koel is so lazy that she lays her eggs in the nests of other birds. So they are fed and brought up by someone else. My brother was no brother. He was an impostor who threw me out of my own home!'

'So the only chick that I brought up was no crow?' asked Co-co sadly.

'No, Co-co. No crow at all,' said Drongo.

'I must find Kau'a and you must tell him this!' she said.

'I will help you,' said Drongo. 'But you must help me find Lori.'

'Once we find Kau'a,' she promised, 'he will find your friend. He's the smartest bird in the forest!'

Not as long as I'm around, thought Drongo.

So Co-co and Drongo flew from village to village looking for Kau'a. There was no sign of him, but they were not discouraged. They spent the days foraging—Drongo feasted on the insects that flew in the fields, and

Co-co scavenged for the scraps that people threw away. They spent the evenings trading barbs near village fires, where she would make fun of his constant tail-swishing.

'Stop that constant flicking of your tail! Like a swizzle stick,' Co-co would say.

'And yours? Thick as a brick,' Drongo would retort.

'Drongo, you're such a dandy,' Co-co would say. 'So vain about your tail. And moustache!'

'Not as proud as you are of your collar,' Drongo would respond.

'At least I have one!' Co-co would crow.

'Keep it down. Your voice could wake baby elephants,' Drongo would reply.

And so on.

Drongo tried to teach Co-co to imitate other birds, but she just couldn't and anyway, she just didn't see the point.

'Christ! You know, it ain't easy,' she'd say.

'You know, how hard can it be?' he'd reply.

The way things were going, very hard indeed. But one day, they saw a little girl playing near the edge of the village. Drongo decided it was time to show Co-co what a little mimicry could do. He made a call like a lost kitten. The little girl wandered out, looking for the cat. He kept calling and moving further and further into the forest. The girl followed, looking under each bush, around every tree and up too, in case the kitten was stuck there. Just when she was far enough from the village, he started making strange guttural sounds. The girl's eyes widened in fear.

Suddenly, Drongo was reminded of Lori and he felt sorry for her. He flew into view quickly and repeated the sound. The girl was surprised to see him, and she hurriedly ran back to her village. Drongo thought to himself that he had gone soft. Maybe his wronging days were over.

But Co-co was convinced now. She started imitating the sounds she heard and found that she was particularly good at the noises that she heard near people. The little girl knew by then that it was the two birds and would come out calling to them. She would make sounds and they would mimic her. Drongo was better at most, but Co-co was not far behind. Co-co would say 'hello' and the girl would giggle with glee.

The little girl would bring scraps of food from home that she threw to the crow. She also figured out Drongo's dietary preferences and even brought him a caterpillar or two. With her encouragement, they produced an endless stream of forest sounds. They stayed in the village a while, playing voice games with the little girl. And soon it became a duet, a duel of long scything notes, of short stabbing trills, of blunt hammer blows.

They greeted other birds with a bewildering array of song that not everyone appreciated. It was widely agreed that Don was supremely talented, but some thought that Co-co didn't quite have the voice for it. Co-co was, of course, undeterred.

'Say hello, Drongo—it's only polite,' she would say when they met someone new. But as extraordinary as Drongo was at imitating the birds of the forest, he could not say 'hello'. He could manage a cheery 'hey', but that was about it.

'Hello, hello, hello!' she would crow.

'Keep it down. Your voice could wake baby elephants,' Drongo would reply.

Until one day, she did. The little giant charged at them, trumpeting a temper tantrum. Co-co and Drongo flew up and perched above, laughing.

'No one ever lets me sleep!' the baby elephant said grumpily. 'Not my mother, not my grandmother, not my aunt, nor my grand-aunt!'

'Maybe you sleep too much!' Co-co laughed.

'You sound just like that other nasty crow,' the baby elephant grumbled. 'Always waking me up. Do you do it on purpose?'

'Yes, we do,' Co-co said. 'It used to be a game that Kau'a and I used to play.'

Co-co and Drongo thought of it at the same moment.

'Where did you last see this nasty crow?' they asked Grumpy.

'Oh, I don't know,' the grouchy little giant said. 'Somewhere in the forest.'

'You must remember something!' Co-co pleaded.

'Nope,' said the big baby, sulky as ever. Drongo, of course, knew how to fix this.

'Little Trumpet,' he started. 'You're really big for your age!'

The baby elephant looked at him suspiciously.

'And I believe you have the best memory in the forest,' he continued. 'Even for an elephant. Now, I bet you really do remember where you saw that nasty crow. We just want to scare him awake too.'

Groucho gave in grudgingly. He remembered crossing the hill with the slippery slopes that he had slid down, nearly tumbling over, and at the end of it, receiving not a reassuring rub from his mother, but a resounding thump on his rump. He remembered the clump of trees on the other side, behind which he had tried to push a bush over—like he had seen his grandmother do with big trees—but the bush had pushed back. He remembered the path along the river from which he had drunk with his trunk for the first time. Before then, he would just bend down on his knees and slosh water directly into his mouth. But the stream was narrow and rocky, and so he'd drunk like his mother, sucking water into his trunk. But he'd been worried about sucking in a frog by mistake.

'Ha ha, you'll have a frog in your throat!' Co-co laughed, and the glum jumbo looked ready to sulk again.

'It's his nose, not his throat, Co-co,' Drongo said. 'And anyway, *you* always sound like you have a frog in your throat.'

That pacified the baby beast. Finally, he remembered the waterfall at the base of the mountain. That was where the herd had stopped a few days earlier. That was where he had been sleeping so peacefully, the sound of the water such a soothing lullaby. Till the crazy crow had flown right up to him and cawed in his ear.

'It's just a game, Jumbo,' Drongo said. 'They don't mean any harm. Just sneak up on the next crow and trumpet loudly in his ear!'

Leaving a slightly cheerier trumpeter tooting behind, Drongo and Co-co set off.

'It's deep in the heart of the jungle, Drongo,' Co-co said. 'Kau'a must really have wanted to hide from me.'

Finding the waterfall was not easy. Or rather, it was easy enough to find a waterfall. Just not *the* waterfall. They found a noisy one, a quiet one, a shy one, a garrulous one. One that gurgled, one that guffawed. One that cackled like a witch. Another that crackled like a villain. Co-co was getting frustrated, Drongo impatient.

And then they found the stream that flowed down the hill, leaped from a ledge above and dived into the pool below. It was beautiful, serene, calm—and not one bird call broke the silence. But still no sign of Kau'a.

Co-co was disappointed, Drongo despondent. This was getting him nowhere in his search for Lori.

Drongo flew around aimlessly for a while, and then up to the top of the waterfall. The stream that ran down the hill was flanked by dense undergrowth on both sides, tangled branches hanging over the middle. He knew that little bushchats and stonechats hopped from rock to rock by the sides of such streams, but he hated the habitat. Too much danger of snagging his precious racket-tails on something.

And all of a sudden, Drongo heard Lori's plaintive squeal. Without a second's thought, he launched himself through the foliage, diving under the branches, skimming over the water. And he heard it again, closer, closer. Till it was right in front of him. No, above! And he looked up, only to find another drongo. Bronzo, a cousin.

'What on earth are you doing that for?' Drongo demanded, his tails swishing with annoyance.

'Doing what?' Bronzo asked cautiously.

'Making that call. The one that my friend Lori makes!' Drongo complained angrily.

'Oh, that. I didn't know that she was your friend,' Bronzo said. 'I just learnt it from her.'

Drongo's anger evaporated. 'Where? *Where?*' he sputtered.

Bronzo pointed up the hill. 'She's winding her way down with her friend. Another loris. I believe they are looking for some monkeys.'

Drongo's heart sank. Had Lori replaced him already? And what was this about monkeys? It didn't make any sense.

Forgetting all about Co-co, he flew up the slope, calling to Lori. Along the river, never losing track of it, as it bounded forward and bent backwards. No call came from up ahead, though, and Drongo wondered if this was another false alarm. And then—as if it was coming through a long tunnel—Drongo heard a call, which was answered. But not by him. Two of them. *It must be the lorises*. With a rush of emotion, Drongo flew towards the sound.

Welcome to Keralafonia

Lori and Boris had been slowly winding their way towards the plateau below. Boris was looking for the McAaque family. They lived deep in the jungle, and knew everything that went on in the forest. They had lived in the heart of the forest for years and years, and knew its darkest secrets. They tom-tommed it to each other, so that if one Mac knew something, everyone did.

When the lorises were just halfway down, they heard the whooping calls of the Macs reverberating over the treetops and up the hill.

'Not too far now, Lori,' Boris said. 'We should reach them in a day or two.'

But it still seemed a very long way down. Lori and Boris separated to forage and after a while, she called to him and he answered. Not a moment later, there was another reply. She started, for she knew it wasn't Boris. Could it be that silly Bronzo? But no, there was a note in the call that she knew particularly well. It couldn't possibly be.

There it came again, as if from the end of a long tunnel! From her perch on the tree, she peered into the dark passage that carved itself through the chaos of foliage above the river. Lori called and heard her own voice lose itself in the darkness. And like a glimmer of hope at the end of the tunnel, a voice came wafting back to greet her. The calls went back and forth till they merged in the middle into a little pool of sound. And just when it seemed like she would drown in the voices, Drongo flew into view.

Time stopped for both of them, and they looked at each other as if it was the strangest dream they had both ever been in. And then they snapped awake.

'Oh my God, Lori! I've been looking for you everywhere,' Drongo said, flapping around her, giddy with delight. If Lori had let him, Drongo would have said a million words—snappy, happy, sappy, soppy—and even that would not have been enough. But all that and more was in her eyes already. And so they just sat there for a few minutes, Lori's liquid look and Wrongo's ravishing rackets saying more to each other than words ever could.

And they may have sat there for a long time, but they heard a gruff clearing of a throat and turned to see Boris watching them, a touch curious and a tad bemused.

'Oh, Boris,' Lori said. 'This is my friend, Drongo. The one that I'm always talking about.'

Boris was not sure whether to be happy for Lori or annoyed by the new arrival, a rival for her affections.

'Ah, the brainy bird,' he muttered. 'Delighted that you found us.'

Drongo beamed. Then he said, 'What happened, Lori? I couldn't believe that awful owl dropped you. I never thought you would survive!'

'And yet you came looking for me,' she said.

'Yes. I got a clue from a mouse, and that's all I needed,' Drongo said, and told her how the mynah mob had created a diversion for him to enter the valley. 'But *how* did you survive the fall?'

'Well, Drongo, if I hadn't thought of you in the moment when I was falling, I wouldn't be here,' Lori said, and told him the rest of her story. Of meeting Boris. And seeing the mystery cat again.

They heard another throat-clearing from the other side. Both turned to see Co-co sitting on the branch, at first furious, then a spot amused.

'Well, you two, are you going to sit here all day long, exchanging these amazing adventures and loving looks?' she asked gruffly.

'Oh, no,' said Drongo. 'Co-co, I'm sorry I left you behind! How did you find us?'

'Oh, it wasn't hard to follow your squeals,' she said. 'I was tempted to just let you go. But I figured you still owe me, and have to help me find Kau'a.'

'I will, Co-co,' Drongo told her. And turning to Lori and Boris, he said, 'This is Co-co, a friend who's been helping me look for you. I have to help her find *her* friend now.'

'Anyone else missing a friend?' Boris asked snarkily.

'Kau'a was at the pool but he left a few days ago. He couldn't have travelled far,' Co-co said, ignoring him.

'Well, then, let's go and find him quickly,' said Drongo. 'Once you two are reunited, I can join Lori and Boris and we can continue our search together.'

'We're going to meet the McAaques,' Lori told Drongo. 'Boris thinks the monkeys may be able to solve the mystery.'

Promising to meet them soon at Monkey Point, Drongo left with Co-co.

Lori and Boris continued their downward journey, the deep and booming calls of the McAaques getting louder and louder. As they got closer, they could hear the drumming of their voices. They sang of the deep, dark jungle and the cool breeze in their hair. And what hair it was—a great shock of silver in contrast to the glistening black of their bodies. Lori looked at them in wonderment. They were majestic, from their magnificent mane all the way to the tip of their lion-tuft tail.

'Welcome to the jungle,' said Antlion McAaque, a tough little monkey.

'Welcome to Keralafonia,' said Beelion, getting straight to the point.

'Welcome, my friends, welcome,' said Sealion, the one with the tricks.

Dandelion just sat there looking pretty.

And in the middle of the group, sat a crow with a gleam in his eye. Lori was astonished. *This couldn't be!*

'Anything is possible here,' said the McAaque at her side. She hadn't realized she had spoken aloud.

'You can't be . . . Kau'a,' she said hesitantly to the crow.

'And why is that?' the crow asked breezily.

'Well, it would be too much of a coincidence!' she said.

'Don't you mean *crow*-incidence?' said the McAaque to her left.

'What coincidence?' asked the crow, ignoring the pun.

'We just met Co-co—she's been looking for you everywhere!'

'Technically that's a co-co-incidence!' said the McAaque to her right.

'Oh, for the love of gordonflies!' she said crossly. These McAaques could be a pain.

But Kau'a was not interested in hearing about Co-co. Meanwhile, Boris had struck up a conversation with some of the McAaques. The monkeys were very difficult to understand. They spoke strangely. They talked of things that Boris knew (or cared) little about. And they talked in ways that sounded wrong but fun. Of course, Boris had been with them before, and so he had some idea of what they *verr saying*.

They were eating some very fermented fruit and holding forth on a series of topics. Antlion appeared to be quite the expert on ambush. He talked at length about how he would lay a trap for a fruit, a carefully crafted cone that an unsuspecting pome might roam into. Beelion was abuzz with her navigation skills. She droned on about the various ways of finding a fruit tree. She tried explaining them by drawing figures of eight and wiggling her bottom, but everyone just looked puzzled. Sealion juggled some berries before diving into a mound of leaves and disappearing. Dandelion drifted off dreamily. It was greatly entertaining, but Boris simply could not get a word in to ask if they knew who the strange cloudy cat was.

'I don't know what happened between you two, but Co-co can't be so bad if Drongo likes her,' Lori was saying to Kau'a. 'He really only likes very smart animals.'

'She is very smart,' Kau'a admitted.

'In fact, I don't know why Drongo hangs out with me,' Lori said. Kau'a looked into the chocolate pools of her eyes and knew why. 'You have to forget about what happened, Kau'a,' she said. 'You have to look for her!'

'And what are you looking for, Lori?' asked the crow.

'Oh, me—I'm just looking for a mystery creature,' said Lori, describing the foggy feline, the cloud of cat.

'Oh, yeah,' said Kau'a, 'I know that animal.'

You could have knocked Lori over with a feather. Now, this was generally true anyway, but particularly at this moment. There she was, a hundred miles—*a hundred miles*—away from home, having nearly lost her life, her friend, and looking for this crazy creature. And Kau'a's answer was so quick, so casual.

'*What?*' she spluttered. 'What is it? Wait, don't tell me. No, do! No, Drongo should be here . . . Oh, do tell!'

Kau'a paused, counting. Do, don't, do, don't, do . . .? 'Sorry, Lori, I just lost track. Did you end on a do or a don't?' he asked finally.

Lori called out to Boris, who was delighted to get away from the monkey conference.

'Tell us,' he said firmly after Lori had filled him in.

Kau'a told them of his experiences since he had left Co-co. He had flown around, distraught at having lost his chicks and distressed about leaving her. He had flown west, where the villages grew bigger and smokier and noisier. In one of them, he came across a catlike animal in a cage. He had seen animals in cages earlier, and would have ignored it as he had done before. But this animal was going to have babies. And Kau'a was sad about losing his own.

He'd waited till it was dark and flown down. He'd taken a closer look at the cat, but it was no cat. Less plain than Panther, less cloudy than Clouded Leopard. Smaller than Siruthai, larger than Leopard Cat. *What was she?*

'I am here to open the cage,' Kau'a had announced.

The animal had looked at him with distrust.

Kau'a shrugged. 'Once the cage is open, it's up to you,' he said.

There was a lock and a lever, but Kau'a was clever. He pulled the lever down, turned it sideways and twisted it up, and pulled at it till the latch fell open.

The animal pushed tentatively and stepped out of the cage. She looked around, wondering if it was just another trap. Finally, she decided to make a break for the forest.

'What's your name?' Kau'a had called after her. But she had already disappeared.

Soon enough, he had heard a commotion as people discovered the empty cage. There had been more noise and yelling, and a few people had followed the animal into the forest. But not for long. Kau'a had decided that place was not pleasant by far. Plus, he was now guilty of a crime. He'd decided that he would hide from Co-co deep inside the forest.

'We see her once in a while,' said one of the McAaques.

'Do you know where she lives?' Boris and Lori asked together.

But of course the McAaques didn't. They looked like princes and spoke like kings, but they were easily distracted.

'I know someone who may know,' said Kau'a. 'When I was at the Nearly Dead Pool at the base of the mountain, I met her once. Or twice. No, once—just once—and this is important.'

'Who?' asked Boris and Lori together.

'The oracle,' Kau'a said. 'You know, the turtle who knows everything.'

'That's just a myth,' said Lori.

'Well, that's what I thought too. Till the time I spent several days hanging out around the pool. I had been hiding from Co-co when a herd of elephants passed by.' A gleam appeared in Kau'a's eye as he recalled waking the poor baby every time he took a nap.

'And when they had gone, one day I heard this rustling in the leaves. At first I thought it was a snake, but it was *very* slow. And steady. I didn't get too close, but I watched from a distance. And finally she emerged. The turtle who knows everything.'

'Well, Kau'a, aren't you quite the encyclopedia? Let's go and meet her,' Boris said.

'Fortunately, it's not far. Lead on, Kau'a,' said Lori.

She was excited. Life had been but a series of dramatic incidents over the past few days. But her desire to find the fuzzy feline remained a constant. From Owli to Boris and now Kau'a, she seemed somehow to co-opt them in her quest to remain connected to the cat. Now she thought she knew why. Drongo had always been the smart one, the one she depended on. This time she wanted to be the one to solve the mystery.

Drongo, meanwhile, sat flicking his racket-tails while his whiskers twitched ominously. They had hunted high and low for Kau'a but had not found a trace.

'A question, Co-co,' he said finally. 'Something's been at the back of my mind. I never asked you how you knew for sure that Kau'a had been at the pool and when he'd left.'

'Oh, when you were off exploring the waterfall, I heard some rustling in the bushes. I found a turtle who has lived near the pool her whole life. She told me she had seen Kau'a, as Groucho had, but that he left when the elephants did.'

'Hmm,' said Drongo, the machinery between his ears whirring away. 'Setting aside this business of Kau'a for a minute, I wonder if she would know who our mystery creature is.'

'Can't that wait?' asked Co-co peevishly. 'You've already abandoned me once for Lori.'

'Oh, we'll search for Kau'a for sure,' said Drongo. 'But doesn't it pique your curiosity too?'

Co-co couldn't help being intrigued. 'I guess it won't take too much of our time to check back and ask her,' she said.

'It's not far. Lead on, Co-co,' said Drongo, the glimmer back in his eye.

What he hadn't admitted even to himself right up to this very moment was that he was more than just a bit eager to find the fleeting feline before Lori. Sure, he had been distracted by her disappearance, distraught at her possible death, determined to discover what had happened. But now that all that was behind him, he felt he should be the one to solve the mystery. He was, after all, the smart one.

They went looking for the turtle.

Viji had led a sheltered existence her entire life. Which may have been forty or fifty or sixty years. She didn't really remember. If she thought back, she could remember a time she could remember a day when she remembered a night on which she had come to live under a tree by the bush beside the pool. She'd feel adventurous on some days and walk all the way to the water. At other times, she pottered around in the leaf litter and stayed extremely still when she saw or heard anything.

Which meant no one—almost no one—ever saw or heard her. Most forest folk even forgot she was there. But she knew they were there. And she watched each one come and go. She knew when Moorhen awoke, and when Frogmouth went to sleep. When Warbler arrived in the winter, and when Shama sang in the summer. When elephants came and elephants went, and never saw her point of view. Some said Viji

was there at the beginning and would be there at the end, but she didn't know of what.

Now there was a sound. And Viji went quiet. She tucked her head back into her shell and drew her feet in as far as they would go. She waited and waited, as she was wont to do. When she poked her head out after a long time, there was that crow again. Darn! She wasn't in the mood to talk to any crows. But, wait—this time there were two other animals with him. Two small animals with kind big, round eyes. Viji knew them—they ate the same food as she did. Bugs and beetles.

But before they could start a conversation, two other visitors arrived. Yes, the other crow that had been looking for this crow. And a bird in a suit. What now? Viji sensed tension in the air and dived under the leaves. There was a lot of noise; the crows were cawing at each other.

'You have to hear this story,' one of them said. There was more cawing.

'I've never heard such nonsense!' the other said later.

And they went back and forth. She heard Lori's plaintive appeal to them to stop fighting. She heard Drongo trying to explain what had happened. She heard Boris getting bored and groaning.

Finally Kau'a said, 'Wow. I'm not sure I believe a bird with such fancy feathers, but it's so far-fetched that even he couldn't have made it up. No one's that creative.'

To which Drongo piped up with, 'Actually I *could* have made it up.'

'Drongo, be quiet!' said Lori. 'That's not helping!'

'Oh, that Drongo thinks he's so clever,' said Kau'a.

'That's because I am,' Drongo was about to say, but he felt Lori's liquefying look on him and he paused. There was a moment of silence, during which Kau'a and Co-co made peace. And then Viji heard one of them say, 'Where's the turtle?'

Darn! She was hoping they had forgotten about her.

Viji poked her head out of the foliage and said, 'Okay, so what do y'all want?'

Lori explained their problem—the mystery cat that kept disappearing before they could figure out what it was. Each time they caught but a fleeting glimpse. And when they thought they'd caught the moment—something to commit to memory—it slipped away, a shifting shape, a wisp of cloud sifted through a palm.

'When you want to catch something that moves, you must sit very still,' Viji said.

That sounds like Owli, both Drongo and Lori thought. They asked, 'But where must we sit?'

'Sit by the pool. Some cat walks by every Sunday, but I'm short-sighted. Can't make out who it is.'

And so they sat and waited. Night fell, the moon rose, some clouds passed by. Boris and Lori peered into the darkness with their big binocular eyes. Drongo sat still, his tail-flick frozen in anticipation. The crows were going a-one, a-two, a-one, a-two, a-three, a-one, a-two, a-one, a-two, a-three. Only the turtle was at peace. Nothing was that important.

The group was crackling with tension, then soggy with boredom. Time dragged its feet in the mud. Boris had his eyes open, but Lori suspected that he had fallen asleep. Drongo's wires crackled a few more times, then snapped, then buzzed a bit and finally went quiet. Even the crows had stopped counting.

And at that moment, into the shaft of moonlight that fell by the pond by the mountain, walked the magical mystery; the misty, mythical, mystical mammal; the fleeting, fading, fleeing, furry, fantastic feline; the shape-shifting, strange secret; the crazy cloud of cat.

'Oh!' said Viji. 'That's not a cat at all. That's Mala.'

With a Little Help from My Friends

A branch protruded from the tree that hung over the water falling from the rock to the pool below. Mala crouched at the end of the branch and leapt to the ledge beside it, then landed lightly on the clump of grass below. She was wary these days. After all she had been through, she kept very much to herself. And soon there were going to be cubs. The moment Mala felt a hint of a gaze upon her, she melted away.

As she moved towards the water, she felt strange. Her instinct was to glide into the darkness, but the situation was peculiar. She felt her senses tingle, but there was no direction in which she could disappear. She felt eyes everywhere. Was she going to be trapped again? Tensed up, she looked around.

Sure enough, she was surrounded. By two crows, two lorises and a drongo. Wait, there was that turtle

too—the one she walked past every week, the one who thought that Mala couldn't see her. Mala was confused. Should she run? Should she hide? Should she scare the daylights out of this tiny audience?

But then she recognized one of the crows, the one who had set her free. And she stopped.

The turtle spoke. 'Mala, you don't know me, but I know you.'

'I know you, turtle,' Mala said in her low, gruff voice.

'Good,' said Viji, noting that she needed to lie even lower in the logs. 'This group wants to talk to you. Don't ask me why, but could you just humour them?'

Lori spoke and Mala turned to her. 'I've been seeing you everywhere I go, Mala! But first, who are you?'

'I'm a civet,' she told them, 'from Malabar. It's at the end of the land the monkeys call Keralafonia.'

'*Ooohhh*,' they all said. A civet! Like Toddy. But so much bigger! Who'da thunk?

'There are very few of us,' Mala said. And then she added, 'I think. I just haven't met many others. I've been in a cage nearly my whole life—till this crow set me free.

'Thank you,' she said, looking at Kau'a, who nodded, embarrassed at suddenly being the good guy.

'And why were you in our forest?' asked Drongo, adding quickly, 'Not that we object or anything.'

'Well,' she said, 'as you can tell, I'm going to have cubs.'

'Sweet! Mala bambinos,' said Co-co.

'And I wanted to get far away from the traps and the cages and everything that might harm them.'

The group nodded in agreement.

'But everywhere I went, there was some danger.'

'What about the valley we saw you in?' asked Lori.

'That was perfect,' said Mala, 'but I overheard a mouse talking about a deranged owl and I had second thoughts.'

'Give us a moment,' said Lori.

Lori conferred with Drongo, then Boris, then Drongo again. Kau'a and Co-co listened for as long as was polite, and then started whispering about building a new nest together. Viji the turtle crawled under an old leaf to take a nap.

Finally, Lori turned to Mala. They had decided that the cup of the valley by the hill with the hump was the safest place for Mala to have her cubs. But the problem of Baba Brown had to be solved. And there was only one way to solve it. M. Owli had to be brought into battle again.

'I will go and call him from his mountain,' Drongo said. 'I will tell him that it's the only way we can all return home safely.'

'Why on earth did he go there?' Boris asked.

'Because the mountain wouldn't come to him?' Drongo snapped. 'I don't know. Who knows why owls do what they do.'

'I will come with you,' Kau'a said. 'You might need the help.'

Boris and Lori decided that they would go up the hill with Mala, where they would wait till they were sure the coast was clear. Co-co would keep them company. Drongo and Kau'a flew back up the mountain, by the side of the hill with the hump, across the low forest and the river and to the cluster of boulders. At the very top was a giant rock. Drongo flew up and was shocked by what he saw.

A grey ghost in the moonlight, a gaunt, sallow owl sat still atop the monolith. A shadow of himself, the owl had turned pale in his penance. He was but a shape at the centre of a smooth, cool stone; the polished black slate shimmered in the moonlight as though it might swallow whole anyone that might sit upon it. Grey glass mirror, viscous cold lava—flowing around the owl but never touching him. Owli sat or floated or hovered on the rock—it was hard to tell which. His eyes were closed, or were they?

He sensed them before they appeared. And said, 'I've renounced the world, Dronko. Do not try to change my mind; my mind is beyond changing. My change is beyond minding.'

'What does he mean?' Kau'a asked.

'Oh, for heaven's sake, Mr O,' Drongo said. 'We have a serious situation here, do you mind?'

'As I said,' said the owl, 'no. And who is this?'

'This is our friend Kau'a,' said Drongo. 'He's a very capable crow.'

'Oh, Don Crow and Dron-Ko. What a nice pair. If your feathers are black, the fool will follow.'

'*What is he saying?*' asked Kau'a, thinking that he had never come across such nonsense but afraid to say so in case it really was profound.

'Mr O, I found Lori,' Drongo said, flying in front of the owl and waving his rackets as if to snap Owli out of his state. 'And we found the mystery cat—well, civet—but, you know, we've found her and they're all coming back up the mountain. But first, we need you to deal with Baba Brown.'

'*What?* Lori isn't dead?' Owli asked disbelievingly. 'The kebab is alive?'

'And well,' said Drongo, 'and waiting for you to make amends for dropping her like-that!'

'Well,' said Owli, 'I suppose I do owe her that. And I suppose that Brown Babu does need a beating. But first, I must eat.'

M. Owli rose from his rock and descended upon the denizens of the forest below, and ate like he had not eaten for days. Drongo and Kau'a followed at a safe distance. Somewhere over the oxbow, they heard a mouse squeak, 'Oh, for heaven's sake, is there no part of this forest that is safe from crazy owls?'

Finally, Owli was ready. 'Let's go,' he said to them, and they led him to the passage between the mountains where Brown sahib ruled. M. Owli was all pumped up and ready. But there was no sign of the other owl. Drongo expected him to appear suddenly and attack them, but even though they flew around in plain sight, he did not appear.

They waited through the night and through the following day. Drongo was worried. If Baba didn't appear soon, there was every chance that Owli would get bored and leave. In search of mice, mountains, merriment. To add to that, Lori and Boris and Mala would be here soon. And her bambinos soon after. They would be alone and exposed and vulnerable, should Baba Brown return to wreak vengeance upon them.

How to summon an errant owl? Drongo's tail flicked, his whiskers twitched and a familiar glint appeared in his eye. Of course, like you called anyone else! By wronging them.

The sun was going down in the west and he could imagine it casting a warm glow on two slender lorises, one cocky crow and one cloudy civet.

'Wait here,' he said to Kau'a and Owli. 'I shall bring Baba Brown to you.'

'Are you going to send him an invitation, then?' Kau'a asked sarcastically.

'In a manner of speaking,' said Drongo, 'a voicemail.'

Before they could respond, Drongo had flown off, and the last thing Owli saw were his rackets twirling dangerously behind him. Drongo remembered now what Mina had said. That Baba had made mice his mortal enemy. That he was attacking and killing them without eating them. Maybe he thought he could get back at Owli by wiping out his food. A bit far-fetched surely, but who knew what he was doing.

Drongo perched at the edge of a clearing and cleared his throat. He then mimicked Mina Mouse. A high-pitched squeak followed by a few *pip-pip-pip*s and another long squeak. Mina telling a story about cheese and terror, about terrible cheese. Nothing moved in the forest. Drongo flew a short distance, perched out of sight and called again. He criss-crossed the forest, sounding out Mina's squeaks and squeals. Where was Baba?

Finally, in desperation, Drongo called like Lori. It was more out of boredom than the belief that it would work. But then he heard wings resonating through the air. Why the sound of the loris had woken Baba Brown, Drongo would never know. Maybe he had fixated on the animal with whom he had last seen Owli.

Flying low through the forest so that Baba could not see him, Drongo flew back to Owli, calling at periodic intervals. He could hear Baba's wingbeats getting closer and closer. If Drongo made one mistake, it would be all over for him. Suddenly, and surprisingly, they came to the clearing in the forest. Drongo was taken by surprise. He was trapped in the open. It was just for a few seconds, but it was enough for Baba Brown to catch a glimpse of him.

Turning briefly, Drongo saw an owl, deranged already in his hunt for the loris and even more enraged at the thought of being wronged. The owl swooped into the trees with a burst of energy. Drongo was quick, but Baba was gaining on him. Where was Owli? Had he wandered off to grab a snack? Drongo ducked under a branch and at that instant, he snagged one of his rackets on a trailing twig. There was nothing for it but to pull free, and he felt the feather break off. Even at that moment of crisis, an angry owl looming large in the corner of his eye, Drongo could not help but feel a pang as he saw in his mind the feather float to the forest floor.

The moment was brief. He felt Baba's powerful wingbeat, the rush of air upon him, as the owl prepared himself to grab him in his talons, to crush his spirit and then his bones, and leave a crumpled black bird behind, an inkblot on the ground. Baba flapped one final time and the force of the blast carried Drongo forward, inches out of the owl's reach. But Baba needed only one more second. His talons curved around Drongo.

Drongo waited for the final moment, his neck tingling with the anticipation of a talon. But it never came. Instead he heard a great commotion behind. Like a stealth fighter, Kau'a had dived through the canopy and struck Baba a second before he'd had his quarry.

Baba was momentarily diverted, but he turned quickly to attack and devour this new enemy. But where there had been a relatively small black crow, there was now a large owl. Baba and Owli faced each other. Drongo, not entirely sure how he had escaped, found a perch to rest on and turned to watch the owls. Kau'a watched from another.

A drumbeat of thunder accompanied the battle as lightning rent the sky.

Baba Brown and M. Owli went hammer and tongs at each other. The tangle of feathers was so thick that Drongo could not tell where one owl ended and the other began. The screeching ripped a tear in the fabric of the evening. Drongo thought that the end of the world must sound something like this.

It was one owl's rage against another's passion. The older owl had never forgiven the younger one for his humiliation. Seeing his swagger had only made him angrier. This time he would finish the job. But the younger owl was no slouch. He was still swifter of step and sharper of mind. And bigger and stronger than he used to be.

Drongo and Kau'a flew from one perch to another, unable to take their eyes off the spectacle. Finally, in a fluid move, Owli feinted one way, flew another and rose above the other owl. Baba Brown was bamboozled. Owli grabbed him in his talons and felt a shoulder snap. Baba Brown was vanquished. Owli could have finished him then, but he didn't have the heart. He let go and they watched the other owl fly away with difficulty, crooked and ragged, till he disappeared into some trees in the distance.

The eagle-owl landed between the two birds, breathing heavily.

'Baba Brown has left the building,' he announced to no one in particular.

'Well done, Mr O!' said Drongo. 'And thanks, Kau'a, for saving my life.'

'I owed you one for helping Co-co find me,' Kau'a said, then wondered aloud, 'What will happen to Baba Brown?'

'I don't think he can fly any more,' said Owli. 'He'll have to retire, maybe walk around pecking for worms like a chicken.'

Together, they left for the western pass to meet the others. They met them halfway down the slope, labouring up slowly. Owli was still abashed at meeting Lori.

'I'm so sorry I dropped you, Kebab!' he said. 'It will never happen again.'

'It's okay, Mr O,' Lori said. 'It wasn't your fault. Not entirely. Anyway, all's well that ends well. Meet my very good friend Boris.'

Owli nodded and said, 'Boris, pleased to meet you. Any friend of Lori's is a friend of mine.'

'And this,' said Drongo with a flourish, 'is Mala, our mystery friend.'

Owli and Mala eyed each other with suspicion. They nodded, but secretly resolved to keep a safe distance from each other. Owli flew Lori and Boris back up the valley, this time without incident or drama. And Mala settled in a corner of the valley's cup, waiting for her cubs to arrive. Kau'a and Co-co bid them farewell. They would build their nest on a tree near the pool; a quiet, safe tree under which lived a very quiet turtle. Quietly.

'Now that you have company, Lori, I will leave with Mr O too,' said Drongo.

Lori was dismayed. She said, 'But you're my best friend! The hardest part of this whole adventure was losing you.'

'Don't worry, Lori. I'll be back,' Drongo said and swished his racket. That's when Lori noticed.

'Oh, no, you've lost one of your tail feathers!' she exclaimed.

Drongo shrugged. 'It's the price of battle, you know.'

Owli groaned. 'Right, yeah, great fight, well done, you could've taken down Baba all by yourself. Come on, let's go.'

Drongo and Owli left, leaving the lorises on the cinnamon tree. Lori was sad that her friend was gone, but somewhere along the way she had decided that she would stay there.

'I wonder why this feels so much like home,' she said.

Boris paused, then said, 'Because it is, Lori.'

She looked at him with wide eyes, wondering aloud, 'Maybe. Do you think I was born here?'

Boris nodded, and Lori asked, 'And how would you know that?'

'Because I played with you here when you were little,' he said.

The truth dawned on Lori like the winter sun. A dim light of realization, a ray that reflected brightly off a golden nugget of truth and finally a glow that warmed her heart.

'Oh, Boris!' she said, thinking that she wanted to tell Drongo. But maybe not, since he was the one who had always wanted to find his family.

The lorises lived in comfortable companionship on the cinnamon tree. The rains came and went. Drongo spent the monsoon discovering new ways to wrong birds out of their worms. His favourite now was the owl's battle screech he could call on to terrorize the other birds. This often made the entire hunting party drop their catch and run. That wasn't very helpful, as most of the insects escaped before Drongo would clean up. But it was great fun.

Drongo gained a certain notoriety for his role in the events that had passed. As the story went, he had led a posse of lorises to a land far away, hired a couple of crows as his lieutenants, interrogated many monkeys, tracked an all-knowing turtle and found Mala the rare Malabar civet. The rarest animal in their forest. A myth no more. And then of course, there was the Battle of Brown, where he had played no small part, losing a racket in dramatic fashion at a key moment. He had distracted Baba, who had grabbed at his tail, and in that moment, Owli had grabbed him from behind and broken him.

Whether these embellishments were Drongo's or the usual path of a good story, is hard to say. Drongo certainly took no effort to correct them, because it was a good story. He stopped worrying about his family. After all, he was Don Wrongo. He had Mr O for a partner. And Lori for a friend.

When the rains stopped, he went to visit her. They reminisced about their great adventure.

'It all seems so long ago,' Lori said.

'Like yesterday,' said Drongo, who was much more used to repeating the story. 'How's Mala, by the way?'

'She had her cubs. Cute as buttons,' said the button herself. 'They left just a few days ago.'

'Hmm. Lori, that's great! And I'm glad it all ended well. But you know, my whiskers are twitching for something new to do.'

'Why, do you want to lose your other racket too?' Lori asked.

'Ha ha, very funny. But you know me, I can't just sit around,' Drongo said.

'Come with me. I want to show you something,' Lori said after a pause.

They walked and flew through the forest in the cup till they came to the thread of trees that straggled down the side of the mountain. Lori led Drongo to the grassland, climbed over a rock and pointed. Drongo perched on the rock and looked. On the other side, the grass had been uprooted viciously, and the kurinji shrubs trampled down. The ground looked like it had been tilled.

'Panni?' asked Drongo. Pigs could make a pretty decent mess when they decided to poke around.

'Not quite,' said Lori. 'I saw him here once. And he said there was nothing in the grass for him to root around for. He left after giving me some useless advice. And look around, whoever it is has left a trail like a whale's.'

Drongo wondered what a whale was, but there was a more important issue here. He asked, 'A tusker rooting around, then? Gaur goring the ground?'

'I guess, but don't you think it's all a bit far-fetched?' Lori asked and gave him a look, the one that could drown a drongo.

And he said, 'Well, Lori, I guess there's only one way to find out.'

Notes

All characters in this book bear a strong resemblance to real-life counterparts (who fortunately cannot sue me). The events, however, are entirely fantasy or fiction or both. Lorises and drongos have not been known to hang out with each other, nor do owls often condescend to help them. Having said that, the story is loosely based on research and observations in the field.

In the early 2000s, my partner, Meera Anna Oommen, and I spent several months on Great Nicobar Island. I was working on leatherback turtles, and Meera was studying the behaviour of the Nicobar tree shrew, a little-known squirrel-like mammal. She discovered that they are frequently followed by the greater racket-tailed drongo, which feeds on the insects that the tree shrew flushes out. This sort of association is common among birds, where some species feed on the insects on leaves and the bark (glean) while others fly around (sally) and catch prey that escape. What was really interesting in Nicobar, though, was that a sparrowhawk, which one would expect to prey on the tree shrew, also joined the group to feed on the flushed animals.

A small (and somewhat slender) mammal, a drongo and a predatory bird? Slightly strange—but a bit like Lori, Drongo and Owli!

Drongos may really be the smartest birds in the world. Samira Agnihotri has spent a decade studying how and why drongos mimic a range of birds (and crickets and frogs and other animals), and they still surprise her. My former student Hari Sridhar spent many years studying mixed-species foraging groups among birds; and Priti Bangal is just starting her journey with mixed flocks, including a study of the role that drongos play in these groups. Perhaps one day they will find that the drongo has been studying them.

In other news, crows are indeed often parasitized by cuckoos, who lay their eggs in their nests; this has been known to happen to drongos as well. The Malabar civet, the shadowy mystery at the centre of the book, is an endangered—perhaps even extinct—animal that has prompted many recent—but unsuccessful—surveys by biologists to find it in the Western Ghats. On the other hand, the forest cane turtle, previously thought extinct, was rediscovered by a young researcher, J. Vijaya, in the 1980s, and the species was eventually named after her. And mice do, in fact, love cheese.